TRICKY SWEET

Connie Shelton

TRICKY SWEET

Samantha Sweet Mysteries, Book 16

Connie Shelton

Secret Staircase Books

Tricky Sweet
Published by Secret Staircase Books, an imprint of
Columbine Publishing Group, LLC
PO Box 416, Angel Fire, NM 87710

Book layout and design by Secret Staircase Books
Cover images © Andreas Meyer, Makeitdoubleplz, EllerslieArt
First trade paperback edition: October 2022

First e-book edition: October 2022
* * *
Publisher's Cataloging-in-Publication Data

Shelton, Connie
Tricky Sweet / by Connie Shelton.
p. cm.
ISBN 978-1649141064 (paperback)
ISBN 978-1649141071 (e-book)

1. Samantha Sweet (Fictitious character)--Fiction. 2. Taos, New
Mexico—Fiction. 3. Paranormal artifacts—Fiction. 4. Bakery—
Fiction. 5. Women sleuths—Fiction. 6. Easter holiday—Fiction. I.
Title

Samantha Sweet Mystery Series : Book 16.
Shelton, Connie, Samantha Sweet mysteries.

BISAC : FICTION / Mystery & Detective.
813/.54

For the first man who ever loved me—my dad.
I miss you every single day.

Prologue

March 26th

"Whoa, dude, watch it! That's a sharp curve." Jacob's hand hovered over his bag of Doritos, his eyes wide, as Casey overcorrected and the sports car slid on the snowy road. The left rear tire dipped alarmingly off the edge but cocky Casey got it back on the paved surface.

"Just shut up and watch for the turn," Casey said with a grin.

"What's the road called?"

"Winter something Lane ... Winter Park Road ... Hell, I don't remember. It's a cabin up here somewhere. We'll find it."

In the back seat, Benjamin Packard wished, for about the fortieth time, that he'd programmed their destination into his phone instead of trusting that Casey knew what he was doing. Why did he always feel like the nerdiest guy in the group? He'd left the spring break travel plans up to Casey (hey, don't worry, I got this) Hardwick. On the other hand, why couldn't he just let it go, let the plan unfold, as his mother always said?

He glanced down at his screen and saw that he had no bars anyway. Okay, that settled it. They'd have to find the rental cabin without electronic assistance. He jammed the phone into his jacket pocket and leaned back in the seat— well, as much as possible, considering he shared the space with two duffle bags and a huge Igloo cooler. Half the beer was already gone, another factor in their confusion about the directions. And why hadn't he insisted they bring something more nutritious than five packs of hot dogs? *Let it go. Let it go …*

Up front, Jacob Winters made the brilliant observation that the snow was coming down a lot harder now that it was dark outside, and there was a lot more of it up here on the mountainside than there'd been in town. Seriously? No one else had noticed this?

Casey responded by hitting the gas, but even he got a little wide-eyed when the Mustang threatened to go sideways. Benjamin closed his eyes. When he opened them they were rolling forward again, at a slower speed.

Jacob jammed the last of the Doritos into his mouth, crumpled the bag, and tossed it over the seat where it landed at Benjamin's feet. Big dumb lunk, Benjamin thought, picking it up and stuffing it into the cooler.

"There's a light!" Jacob said, pointing up the hill. "Take a left—that's gotta be the driveway for the cabin."

The *driveway* turned out to be about a quarter mile of steep dirt road, which showed up only as a path of white through the dark, lined on both sides by huge pine trees, and not a sign of any other vehicle tracks.

"You sure this is it?" Casey didn't take his eyes off the narrow access.

"Gotta be. The lights are on. Didn't the owner say they'd leave lights on in case we arrived after dark?"

Benjamin had to admit—privately—that he hadn't seen any other lights since they turned off the Taos Ski Valley Road. Jacob could be dumber than dirt, but even he sometimes got things right.

The Mustang's headlights flared through the falling snow and illuminated the façade of a log cabin with a steeply pitched roof as Casey steered into a small clearing. Carved support posts flanked three steps up to a porch where it looked like part of the trim pieces were broken.

"Seems kind of plain, compared to the pictures they showed online," Casey commented. He pulled the car up even with the steps, which had been cleared of snow. "Hey, no worries. We're here. Let's carry the important stuff in and we'll have us another beer and—"

"There's probably even a fireplace where we can roast up a bunch of those hotdogs," Jacob said.

Benjamin swore the big guy was always hungry. Then again, he couldn't argue with the sentiment. It had been hours since they stopped for lunch somewhere along Interstate 40. The heater in the Mustang wasn't the greatest, and his feet felt like blocks of ice. It didn't help when he pried himself out of the cramped seat and stepped into snow that came up to his ankles and filled the tops of his sneakers. He looked down in dismay.

When he looked up again, light spilled out onto the porch. The front door was open and two people stood there staring at them.

"Uh, Casey …?"

Always the leader of the pack, Casey stepped forward and gave the older couple one of his winning smiles, the kind he used with his grandmother. "This is the right place, isn't it? The cabin-share rental?"

The gray-haired woman turned to the man, and some kind of look passed between them. A smile lit her face. "It sure is. Come on in. You boys look hungry."

Jacob was standing with his mouth open; Benjamin glanced uncertainly at the others. Only Casey moved ahead.

"Bring your stuff inside," the old man said. "Supposed to go below zero tonight and you don't want your things to freeze."

"I've got a big pot of green chile stew on the stove, and we'll get you settled in real quick," the lady assured them.

They left their snowboards strapped to the top of the car but reached for their duffle bags.

"You didn't say our rental was shared with anyone else," Benjamin muttered to Casey as he slung his bag's strap over his shoulder.

Casey tossed back a lock of blond hair that hung in front of his eyes. His expression went nonchalant and he shrugged. "I don't know. Hey, there's a hot dinner waiting. Who's complaining?"

Benjamin sighed and patted his pocket to be sure his phone hadn't fallen out. He'd check the details later. Jacob was already up on the porch. The other two followed, laden with bags and boots.

The old man met them at the door. Closer up, he appeared to be practically ancient—seventy, at least. "I'm Lyle," he said. "Wife's name is Nancy. C'mon, let's get you settled in."

He led the way through a small foyer with a living room on the left and dining room on the right. Down a narrow hallway lined with wood paneling, Lyle paused in front of a door.

"There you go. The guest room." He stood aside, effectively blocking the hall and giving the boys no alternative but to go into the room.

It was furnished with a double bed pushed against one wall and a set of bunks against another. Colorful quilts topped all three, and the pictures on the walls looked like something Nancy had most likely painted herself.

"Bathroom's right through there." Lyle pointed to a connecting door. "Lots of clean towels and such. Once you're settled in, come on out to the dining room. Nancy's green chile stew is the best, just what you need when you're cold and hungry."

He pulled the bedroom door shut with a click, leaving them standing there and staring at each other.

"What the hell, Casey?" Jacob stage-whispered. The walls didn't seem all that likely to be soundproof. "You said we'd have our own place. We'd meet girls up at the ski lodge, have a place to bring them, drink all we wanted, spend our spring break partying."

Casey dumped his own duffle on the largest bed. "Chill, dude. We'll figure this out. We probably just got the wrong place."

"Casey—they seemed like they were expecting us," Benjamin pointed out.

"Yeah, so? They have some company coming, and they think it's us. The whole thing's gonna be good for a lot of laughs later. Right now, I'm hungry, and that stew was smelling pretty good. You want to head back out in the weather right now? Let's not blow a chance for a hot meal. I'll call the rental agency and straighten it all out."

Jacob walked into the bathroom and closed the door. Casey pulled out his phone. "Hm. No bars. Well, later."

Benjamin debated about the bunks, deciding he didn't want the hugely overweight Jacob on the one above him, so he snagged the top bunk for himself by plunking his bag and jacket on it.

"We'll meet you in the dining room," Casey called out to the closed bathroom door.

Benjamin checked his own phone. No signal for him either, and it didn't appear there was a wi-fi network available. He'd have to ask.

"Coming?" Casey seemed impatient.

The dining room was warm, the table set for three, and the scent of onions and chile wafted from the kitchen in a way that made them salivate. Nancy carried bowls of steaming stew to the table.

"We ate earlier," she said, sending a grandmotherly smile toward each of them, "but there's plenty left. You boys eat up and feel free to ask for seconds."

Benjamin held up his phone. "I promised my family I'd let them know we arrived safely, but I'm not getting a signal."

Lyle had appeared in the doorway with a basket of biscuits. "Won't get one here, neither. Mountains all around."

"So, you don't have cell phones? Internet?"

"Don't believe in 'em. That's how the gov'ment spies on people."

Ah. "I'd be happy to pay for a call if I can use your landline."

"Later, honey," Nancy said. "Eat your stew while it's hot." She fluttered about, mother-henning them to the chairs.

The food was every bit as delicious as promised, and the young men scarfed it down (three bowls for Jacob). Nancy lingered nearby, offering more iced tea, clearing dishes as they finished. When their stomachs were full and eyelids heavy, she urged them to make it an early evening as she walked them down the hall to their room. They were tired, after all, from the long drive. None of the three had the energy to protest, and within minutes they'd shed their clothes and tucked under the weighty quilts.

Benjamin's last thought was that he'd never managed to find the landline phone. They were completely isolated in an unfamiliar place and no one knew where they were.

Chapter 1

Three days later ...

Samantha Sweet paged through her portfolio of baked delicacies, searching for inspiration for this Easter season. Cupcakes always sold well and, of course, anything chocolate. But how to make them different? Sweet's Sweets had been in business nearly eight years (she couldn't believe it!), and the Taos clientele were loyal beyond measure.

"Whatcha doing?" Jennifer Baca, the young woman who kept the front of the shop in immaculate order, stepped over to the bistro table where Sam sat alone and topped up her mug with their signature blend coffee.

"Looking for ideas. Do you think I'm going stale? My creativity seems at a low point right now."

Jen patted Sam's shoulder. "Stale? Are you kidding? We just came off a Christmas season and Valentine's Day that beat all our sales records. The wedding cake you did for the Stevensons was magical."

Magic. Maybe that's where Sam's energy was lagging. She hadn't handled the wooden box in several weeks, and although the ancient artifact was not exactly meant to be a catalog of pastry ideas, Sam found all of her senses heightened each time the carved box warmed her hands. Back when Beau was still sheriff, she'd even discovered clues to help with his cases.

She realized her mind was drifting when she heard voices from the kitchen. Two seconds later, her daughter appeared, a froth of cinnamon curls escaping her knitted cloche. Kelly was laughing, probably at something one of the bakers had said.

A shriek pierced the air with, "Grammy!" and five-year-old Anastasia raced toward Sam.

"Hey, you two. What's up?"

Ana went into a long and bubbly description of their visit to one of the local galleries, where she'd apparently been given a quick lesson in art history.

"When you're homeschooling, you find chances to teach wherever you can," Kelly said as an aside. Her phone rang just then and she pulled it from her pocket and stared at the screen.

"Can I have a cookie, Mom?"

"One," Kelly said absentmindedly as she touched her phone screen.

Ana raced to the sales counter and asked Jen for her recommendation.

"Hm. Wonder who this is? It's my old area code in California."

"One way to find out," Sam said.

Kelly rolled her eyes and took the call. "Summer?

Ohmygosh how *are* you? *Where* are you?"

A pair of older ladies walked into the bakery just then, and Kelly stepped past them to finish her call outside. Sam picked up her notebook and coffee mug and steered Ana, who now had two macarons in her little fists, toward the kitchen while Jen turned to the customers.

"Help me figure out what cupcakes we should make for Easter this year."

"Bunnies are always a good choice," said the wise-beyond-her-years little girl. "I'd go with bright colors. You know, for variety."

"Brightly colored bunnies—you may be onto something."

The kitchen was bustling with its usual energy. Julio, the baker, was pulling cake layers from the large bake oven and, judging by the sizes, a big wedding must be coming up. Becky Harper stood back from the worktable, critically eyeing a fashion-purse cake, which must be for a young woman's birthday party or bachelorette do. She picked up a sifter and gave the design a very light dusting of gold powder.

"I like the gold," Ana said. "Can I taste?"

Becky reached out and stopped the child's curious finger only a quarter-inch from the cake board. "Uh, not from there." She shook a little of the edible gold powder onto the worktable and allowed Ana to dip her finger and lick it.

"It doesn't taste like anything."

"I know, right? It's all for show." Becky picked up the cake and carried it to the walk-in fridge.

Sam was about to suggest that Ana help her inventory the supplies so they could place an order when Kelly came breezing back in.

"You'll never guess who that was on the phone."

"Summer?"

A sigh. "Well, yeah."

"Sorry, I don't know Summer from California." Sam stood in front of the shelving units that held staples, eyeing the supply to determine what they might be running low on.

"Oh, that's right. I doubt you ever met her." Kelly picked up a blueberry muffin that had somehow missed being delivered to the sales counter. "She and I worked together at Bradwick, which is not important. She was really young and brand new at the time, and because we were the only two females in a man's world, we sort of latched onto each other. Nice girl. She still lives in L.A."

"And she's calling you now because …?"

"Yeah, strangest thing. She remembered I came from Taos and had moved back here."

"And …?"

"Her little brother came out here to spend his spring break snowboarding with some friends, and no one's heard from them."

"Because … young guys don't call home all that often …"

"That's what she thought at first, and she tried to reassure her mother that everything is okay but— I'd better backtrack. Casey was a late-in-life baby for the family. Summer and Casey's father died a few years ago, and their mother has been in a nursing home, not doing well. Casey lives with Summer and her husband. He's in college and doesn't seem to be graduating, just keeps taking more courses, which all sound like they're on the light side—golf, for one. And the two buddies he's traveling with are kind of the same, still living at home well into their twenties."

Sam nodded, knowing but not really understanding this new trend. Her own journey included leaving home the minute she was out of high school, traveling to Alaska on her own, having a baby at a young age, and raising her daughter on her own.

"Summer's mom took a turn for the worse this week, and she's really trying to get hold of Casey to let him know he might need to cut his trip short. Multiple calls and texts have gone unanswered."

"Batteries die, signals don't go through."

"True. Anyway, she first got in touch with the other two families. No one had heard from the boys. Jacob's mother had also tried to get through, with no luck. Benjamin's parents seemed barely aware he wasn't back down in his little man-cave in the basement."

"Did she report this to Evan?"

"I asked that question. Yes, says she did. She felt like everyone kind of brushed her off. That's when she remembered that Beau was sheriff and that I was connected." She held up one hand. "I know. I told her Beau's retired. But, Mom, she sounds so worried. Her mother's situation is getting worse, and this is important to them. And we do know Evan, so I can't say I don't have *any* connections with law enforcement around here. I told her I'd ask around."

"We can do that," Sam said.

"See? I knew you would help." Kelly's smile lit up.

"I may have gray hair, but even I know that three young guys surely all have cell phones and it would be odd for none of them to answer." Sam paused while jotting items on her list. "I need to run to the store for a few things. How about if we do that together and then stop by the sheriff's office and talk to Evan ourselves?"

Thirty minutes later, Sam pulled into the visitor parking area at the county sheriff's department building. After being an insider, Beau's wife and a deputy herself, it felt strange to walk through the front door instead of the one that led directly into the squad room in back. But Evan was as welcoming as ever, ushering them into his office as soon as he heard they were there on business.

Seeing the younger man in Beau's chair was another thing Sam hadn't quite become used to, but she settled into one of the visitor chairs while Kelly outlined the basics.

"Yeah," he said, "yesterday. I followed up, but I guess the lady didn't like the answers."

"Can you fill us in?" Sam asked. "Just so we know what to tell her."

"Sure. Maybe you'll come up with some ideas for me." He moved his computer mouse around until he came to the screen he wanted. "The caller said her younger brother and two friends came up for snowboarding during spring break. They'd arranged a vacation rental through one of those online services but didn't leave any specific information with their families. Your friend only had a confirmation number for the rental but it wasn't an actual link she could follow."

"That agrees with what she told me," Kelly said.

"So, I followed up with the major ones until I got a match to the confirmation number. Which led me to the property address and the owner's name. I called the owner, who lives in Oklahoma, and was told they just assumed the renters had showed up. When they don't hear anything, they figure it's good news, that nothing's wrong with the cabin, the renters' stay is going all right."

Sam nodded, writing down the name and address he showed her in his notes.

"I spoke with TSV police—you know Taos Ski Valley only has forty-some residents, a mayor, a police chief and a couple of officers who mainly call tow trucks for tourists who slide off the roads. Basically, everyone knows everything up there, but none of them knew anything about this group of kids. Sorry—young men. No accident reports involving their vehicle. It was a two-wheel-drive sedan, not exactly ideal for this country, but ..." He scrolled down a bit further. "I even checked with the Forest Service, in case they'd decided to go off into the back country. No indication of that."

"Did you go up to the cabin?"

"Yeah. Buttoned up tight. But that may not mean anything. Curtains drawn, could mean they didn't want anyone peeking in the windows to see their stuff inside. There'd been fresh snow that morning, so any tracks would have got covered up. I couldn't say for sure that no one had been there. Couldn't say they had."

"Neighbors?"

"The cabins up in that area are pretty far apart, at least a couple acres between. And no permanent residents on that road."

"Which means there's no nosy neighbor who watches all the comings and goings."

"Exactly." Evan pushed the mouse aside and folded his hands on the desk. "I feel for the family, and I know your friend is worried, but I've done all I can without initiating a full-on search and rescue mission. From what I can tell, it's just not warranted right now. We don't even know that the boys didn't change their plans and decide to spend spring break in Vegas or somewhere entirely different. They're all over twenty-one."

Chapter 2

March 27th

Casey moaned as he rolled over, pulling the quilt snugly over his shoulders. His head felt like a basketball—hard and round and like it would bounce if it touched anything. How many beers had he drunk yesterday? Not enough to make him feel this crappy.

"Hey, you awake?" came Benjamin's whisper from the top bunk across the room.

"Ugh. I guess so."

"What time is it? I can't find my phone."

The heavy Indian blanket that served as a curtain kept the room dim, but bright light rimmed the edges. Casey reached for the edge of the drape and pulled it aside. Hard, white light blasted his eyes. He dropped the blanket back in place.

"So, daytime," Benjamin added helpfully.

"No shit."

On the lower bunk, Jacob flopped from his side to his back, shaking the bed frame. It knocked against the wood-paneled wall.

"Hey, lazy-butt. You got your phone? What time is it?" Benjamin peered down at the heftier guy.

"What does it matter? We're on vacation, dude." Jacob scrubbed at his face and opened his eyes.

"Yeah, what's with you always needing to know the time?" Casey teased. "Man, it's spring break. We're gonna get our boards and shred the gnar!"

Benjamin closed his mouth. He couldn't explain it either, the way he always kept track of time. It was just a thing he did.

"It was snowing pretty good last night," Jacob said. "Think the old Mustang will get us on up to the lifts?"

Casey waved off the idea. He actually had no idea how the car would handle in snow. Maybe they should have rented a Jeep or something, but he wasn't about to express that worry to his friends. He avoided the need to answer by clearing his throat and coughing, swinging his legs over the edge of the bed and reaching for his pants. He swore he'd left them across the foot of the bed, but when he looked around, he saw that they were neatly folded and draped over a chair in the corner. Each of the other guys' clothing was similarly folded and draped over the footboards of the bunks.

Okay, this was too weird. Had the already-fussy Benjamin gone all OCD after Casey drifted off to sleep? Surely not.

A light tap on the door startled him.

"You boys decent?" came a female voice. The door cracked open an inch or two and the old lady stood there, facing the door frame. "I've got breakfast all ready. Who wants *pancakes*?"

Casey stared. Jacob and Benjamin exchanged a look.

"Um, we didn't realize this was a bed and breakfast," Benjamin said. "We're not quite dressed yet."

"That's perfectly all right," Nancy said. "Just come on in the kitchen when you're ready. The griddle's hot and the batter's all stirred up. I'll make you chocolate chip or blueberry." The door closed and her footsteps retreated down the hall.

"What the hell?" Jacob muttered. "Didn't I come on vacation to get away from my mother?"

Benjamin had sprung down from the top bunk. "Oh, give her a break. She's just a nice lady who wants to make us a treat. It's probably something they do on your first morning here."

He stopped when he saw his clothing neatly folded at the end of the bed, and his glance slid between Casey and Jacob. Discarding the idea that either of his friends would have done it, he kept his mouth shut and began dressing. Another amenity of the cabin?

In the bathroom, their toothbrushes lay in a neat row on the vanity top, each with the correct tube of toothpaste beside it. Benjamin noticed them as he stood at the commode, relieving himself. A prickle of gooseflesh crept up his neck. He'd watched a movie a few weeks ago with his mom, one in which the manservant of the king did stuff like that, waiting on the royal personage, hand and foot. But real people in real life didn't do this.

He finished his business, washed his hands, and messed

up the toothbrush arrangement. Casey would come in here and think he'd set them all in place. And the last thing Benjamin needed was for the other two, the guys from the cool crowd, to start razzing him about being even more of a nerd.

He looked in the mirror, hated the way his short hair lay perfectly in place, and ran damp fingers through it to mess it up. He had to figure out how Casey achieved that tousled look, that casual don't-give-a-shit attitude that made girls gravitate to him.

Later. Right now he could smell bacon cooking.

Jacob was already at the kitchen table, a stack of chocolate chip pancakes in front of him, a jug of syrup in hand, from which he proceeded to pour a small lake onto the plate. A platter holding what must be a full pound of bacon sat in the middle of the table.

"*Good* morning, Benjamin," Nancy called out. "Blueberry or chocolate chip?" She stood poised at the stove, ready to ladle out the batter.

"Blueberry, please." She remembered his name? He couldn't help but feel flattered.

"Take a seat, and I'll bring them right over. Did you boys sleep well?"

Jacob's mouth was full and Benjamin was about to answer when Casey stumbled into the room. At Nancy's query about his choice of pancakes, he came out with, "Coffee. Just coffee."

"Of course. What was I thinking?" She flipped Benjamin's pancakes while reaching to a shelf above for mugs, something like Supermom combined with the waitress who was so good you'd leave a twenty-dollar tip.

Before the pancakes were fully browned, she'd managed

to pour three mugs of coffee from an old-fashioned pot and deliver them to the table. A moment later, Benjamin's blueberry cakes were waiting there too. He sat down and began to give them a lavish swipe of butter.

Casey carried his mug to the window and stood there, staring at the snowscape outside. The kitchen was at the back of the house and the window gave a view of nothing but pine trees and snow.

"We can't wait to get out on the slopes today," Benjamin said, mainly to fill the momentary silence, or to keep Nancy from offering more food.

"Oh, dear," she said.

All three of the guys turned toward her.

"Well, it's just that the wind came up during the night. Not sure how the roads will be."

"How far are we from the chairlifts, anyway?" Benjamin wished, once again, that he'd pressed a little harder for Casey to share details.

"Oh, it's only a couple of miles," Nancy said, carrying the coffeepot around to see who needed refills. "But the drifts, you know. Until the plows get out."

Casey had wandered across to the living room but he returned now, with fire in his eyes. "Where's my car?"

Nancy stood at the stove and it seemed that she froze for a split second before putting her grandmotherly smile back on.

"My damn car! Where's my car?" He slammed his mug down on the table.

A wave of cold air whooshed into the room. The old man stood in the kitchen doorway. "Just simmer down, you young buck. And watch your mouth. My wife's a lady."

"Lyle …" Nancy placed a hand on his shoulder.

"I'll tell you where your car is. I moved it into the barn last night. Wind was coming up and I thought them board-things you had on top might just take right off with it."

"Seriousl—?"

"Go look for yourself out front. Snow's all drifted up to the porch, and until I get my plow out there, no one's going anywhere."

Casey shot him one last defiant look, and Benjamin soothed it over by agreeing that the snow looked pretty deep. Jacob swabbed the last of his pancakes in the syrup puddle and asked for more. The request set Nancy into action once again.

"All right, then. Everybody take a seat and I'll have more pancakes on the table in a second. Honey, I don't want you out there on the plow until you've had a good breakfast. Everything else can wait." She poured batter for another eight pancakes onto the large griddle, then turned to the group. "You'll see. Life just has to slow down a bit when the weather takes over. We do this a lot in the winter, have a late breakfast and then read or watch movies all day."

Even Jacob seemed to realized those were not options for Casey. They'd come here to live it up, not be stuck in a log cabin with these oldsters. But thankfully, he kept his opinion to himself, stuffing his mouth with bacon instead.

Tempers cooled as the pancakes and bacon went down. Twenty minutes later, Lyle pushed his plate back and stood. "Goin' to get the plow. Anyone wants to help shovel the porch is more than welcome."

Casey gave a little chuff, which Benjamin covered by coughing. He had no idea how one went about shoveling a porch, but it sounded like more fun than watching

Jacob stuff his face or Casey stomp around in a mood. But first ... "I told my family I'd let them know when we arrived," he said to Nancy. "Can you show me your landline?"

She led him into the living room and pointed to an old fashioned telephone that had a wire leading to a plug in the wall. "It's the only kind that works if the power goes out."

He picked up the handset and thought a minute to remember his home number before he began to press buttons. "Nothing's happening."

"Did you get a dial tone?"

Dial tone? "I don't hear anything."

She stepped over and took the receiver from him, listening. Set it back in place, picked it up, and listened again for a moment. "You're right. A line must be down somewhere. It's dead."

Chapter 3

So, what do we do next?" Kelly asked. She sat at Sam's kitchen table with a mug of tea, while her mom rummaged in the fridge for dinner ideas. Ana was out in the barn with Grandpa Beau, supposedly to check out their selection of saddles and maybe take a short ride on the gentle, elderly horse.

"I assume you're talking about Summer and her missing brother, not whether I'll settle on pork chops or vegetable soup?"

Kelly sent her a look.

"Well, I'm a little skeptical about Evan's idea that the boys would have changed plans in favor of something as different as Las Vegas. Summer told you they loaded up snowboards and winter clothing. In Vegas, they'd want to dress up, play it cool. That's a big switch."

"Yeah, I got the feeling *Vegas* was just a word that popped out of Evan's mouth. He really meant 'anywhere else in the world.' Don't you think?"

"Probably. Which gives us no clues whatsoever."

Kelly sighed, staring into her tea mug. "I just feel really sad about this. Summer is a good friend. You know the kind, the coworker whose personality just clicks for you. She and I didn't even work in the same office all that long, but we stayed in touch. Met for lunch every week or two after I left Bradwick. Emailed a *lot* since I moved back to Taos."

Sam had one or two friendships like that.

"She's a few years younger than I am, and her little brother—well, I guess Casey's college age now, but he was just the bratty little brother in those years. Except …"

Sam sipped from her own mug, giving Kelly a moment.

"When their dad died, poor little Casey took it hard. The whole family did, but … well, the kid was spoiled rotten and I got the distinct idea most of that was their dad's doing. And their mom switched from disciplinarian to spoiler after he was gone. Summer called it enabling. I tried to offer a neutral, middle ground. What young boy wouldn't be affected by losing his dad, right?"

"So true."

"Anyway, things changed dramatically again with their mom in a nursing home. Summer's got so much on her plate—working, married and raising two kids, and keeping Casey in school while footing most of the bills for all of it. Of course—" she held up one hand "Johnny Gaines makes great money and isn't at all stingy about supporting Summer's extended family too."

"Sounds like she married a good man," Sam said.

"As did both you and I." Kelly smiled and reached out to take Sam's hand.

"I hope we can do something to help."

Boots stomped on the front porch and Sam glanced out the kitchen window to see Beau and Ana.

"Let's run the whole scenario past Beau. Maybe he'll have some ideas," Kelly suggested. She got up to reheat the kettle and dumped a packet of hot chocolate mix into a cup for Ana.

"How was the horseback ride?" Sam asked, as Beau hung his jacket on the rack near the front door. Ranger and Nellie, their Lab and border collie, whined at the door, unhappy about being left outside.

"Fun!" Ana piped up.

"Muddy. Spring." Beau checked the bottom of his boots. "You know how it is after a storm like the one Tuesday night."

Sam knew. Warm afternoons like this one always brought on the beginnings of a thaw. But it would dip below freezing again tonight. The best time to get anything done outdoors was before the sun hit the ground in the morning.

"And we're due to have more snow by the weekend," he added.

Which would start the whole cycle of freeze, thaw, mud, wind to dry things out, then another round of snow or rain. Spring was her least favorite time of year here in the northern mountains.

"Coffee, tea, or chocolate?" she asked, planting a kiss on his cool cheek.

"Coffee. Instant's fine."

They settled at the kitchen table with a plate of

snickerdoodles from Sweet's Sweets, and Kelly related to Beau the phone call from her friend and their subsequent conversation with Sheriff Evan.

"We can't decide what to do next," she admitted. "I feel obligated to do something. Summer was sounding kind of frantic, given her mother's declining condition."

Ana dunked a cookie in her hot chocolate, dribbled a good bit of the liquid down her chin, and spoke up. "If I was really grown up, like in college, I'd want my vacation to be a big adventure. Like, I'd go hiking *waaayyyy* into the forest and make a campfire, and cook s'mores, and I could eat them all day long."

Sam didn't point out that even Ana would be sick of s'mores after three days.

Beau took more of a traditional cop's approach. "Interview the families … find out who saw them last. Maybe there's a trail of credit card charges for gas and food. Maybe they stayed in motels along the way. Although you'd either need to get the families to cooperate and share that with you, or law enforcement would need to get involved with warrants and procedures. If you can follow their trail, you might get information from someone along the way."

Kelly jotted the key words on a napkin.

"When you talk to the families, see if you can learn more details about what the guys packed. You mentioned snowboards. Did they take adequate clothing? Did they pack water, food, camping gear? What kind?"

"Marshmallows!"

He gave Ana a wink. "That would be a good clue, if they packed marshmallows and graham crackers."

"Anything else, Beau?" Kelly sat with her pen poised.

"Have the families send you some photos. You *need* to

know what the missing person looks like. Get a couple of each of the young men, if you can. People always send the studio portrait from the yearbook, but some casual shots would be even more valuable."

Sam felt silly for not having thought of that in the first place.

"Looks like we have our work cut out for us," Kelly said. "Right after dinner, I'll start with Summer and see what she can give us."

"We'll help with making calls too," Sam offered, generously including Beau in the *we*. She picked up the empty mugs and wiped the countertop with a sponge.

Kelly helped Ana into her jacket and picked up her own. "Come by in the morning and we'll see where the interviews take us. I'm getting kind of excited to play detective."

At the front door, Beau gave her a pat on the shoulder and then turned to Sam. "Shall I tell her it's rarely exciting work, interviewing witnesses? It never goes the same in real life as it did for Nancy Drew."

Sam gently shook her head. "Don't burst the bubble just yet."

"Nancy *Drew*?"

"Hey, not saying this isn't serious. It could turn out that way. Could turn out to be a misunderstanding among all these family members. You never know what you'll dig up."

Sam had a feeling those words were the prophetic tip of the iceberg.

Chapter 4

"Oh dear," said Nancy with a sigh. "This happens sometimes. A phone line must be down somewhere. Ice gets on the lines, you know. Especially in these spring storms."

Benjamin set the receiver back in place, feeling a little stunned. He couldn't remember a time in his life he'd been unable to make a phone call. He turned to ask the older woman a question, but she'd already bustled back into the kitchen.

In the front entry, Lyle was dressed in a sheepskin coat and boots, donning a cap with some kind of fur on the earflaps. Casey hovered behind him, seeming woefully underdressed in jeans and a stylish down jacket.

"How long will it take to plow a path out of here?" he demanded of the older man.

"As long as it takes." Lyle yanked the front door open and pulled a glove on his left hand. With his right he fished a set of keys from his coat pocket.

Benjamin watched from the front window as Lyle picked up a wide push-broom and stomped down the two steps to ground level. The snow came almost to his knees. Casey followed him onto the porch, then halted.

Twenty yards away, a metal building with two tall garage doors must be the 'barn.' Beside it sat a hefty-looking black pickup truck with huge tires and a toothy grill, facing the driveway. A red snowplow was attached to the front, all ready to go. Lyle took the broom to the windshield and side doors, quickly clearing a view for himself. He tossed the broom into the bed of the truck, unlocked it, and climbed in. A moment later, the angry beast roared to life.

"He'll have the driveway clear in twenty minutes or so," came Nancy's voice from behind him. "But it won't make a difference until the county gets out here to do the highway and the county road down there." She pointed in the direction he supposed they must have taken when they arrived in the dark last night.

"I suppose. I just don't want my family to worry." But would they? His dad was always wrapped up in work, to the point where he just stayed at the office overnight a lot. His mom, knowing their only kid was away for a whole week, probably took the chance to have dinner out with friends. Or maybe she was entertaining clients—the real estate market was hot right now, and she'd been making the most of it.

"How about your wi-fi?" he asked. "If you can give me the password, I could get an email out to my mom."

"Oh." Nancy paused while drying her hands on a

dish towel. "We don't have internet. Lyle doesn't think it's a good idea to have the equipment in the home. Secret agencies spy on people through those things. Same with satellite television."

Seriously? Benjamin considered himself pretty tech savvy, but the idea that the government would want to spy on ordinary people who lived out in the hills seemed way too farfetched. He could make the argument for installing a virtual private network, cyber-security software, and taking other measures, but he realized this wasn't Nancy's call at all. Lyle ran the show here.

He stared out the front window, watching the old man run the pickup truck back and forth, making aggressive cuts in the snow with the plow. It appeared the new snowfall was maybe four or five inches, but the drifts had piled it up to a foot deep in places. Lyle clearly knew his property well; in a few deft moves he'd made a narrow track to the road before following up by piling the extra snow in great heaps to the sides.

Casey must have realized he needed warmer clothing if he planned to get into the barn and check his car. He came back inside, a scowl on his face, but he accepted Nancy's offer of more coffee. This time he took two strips of bacon and munched on them while he looked out at Lyle's progress.

"Hey guys," Jacob said, emerging from the hallway fully dressed now. "They got some cool vintage video games. Nancy says we can play them on a TV that's down in the basement rec room."

The other guys shot him a look. "We came here to hit the slopes," Casey said.

"If they don't get the main road cleared, we could

still get our boards off the car and fiddle around here, on the property. Maybe?" Benjamin heard how lame that sounded, and Casey's glance out at the thick forest told him that would never work.

"I'll get us out of here." Casey sounded sure of himself, and Benjamin felt a little relieved.

The black truck stopped roaring, and the guys saw that Lyle had backed it into its spot beside the barn.

"Good—he's done," Casey said. "Grab your coats and boots and we'll be up on the slopes in no time."

Benjamin sent a questioning glance toward Nancy but got only a bland look in return.

They geared up with their snow jackets and boots and clomped their way behind Casey, out the front door and down the porch steps.

"Open the garage," Casey told Lyle.

"You gonna try it, huh? I'm telling you—"

"You think I can't drive my own car?" Even Jacob looked a little uncertain. True, Casey was an excellent driver on warm, dry California highways, but this was way different.

Lyle challenged him. "Sure—go ahead and try it." *Smartass.* He pressed the button to raise the garage door, then trudged back to the front porch to watch.

The three guys clambered into the Mustang, Benjamin again jammed into the backseat next to the beer cooler, which they'd forgotten to carry inside last night. Casey cranked the ignition, muttering a little when the cold engine didn't turn over immediately. It started on the third try, coming to life with a satisfying roar.

"Okay, guys, we ready? Boards?"

"Check. On the roof rack."

"Lift tickets?"

Benjamin paused. They'd purchased a package deal online and the confirmation message was on his phone. Surely, he'd get a signal once they reached the actual ski area. "Check," he said.

Casey shoved the shifter in gear and gave the Mustang some gas. On the dry garage floor, traction was firm and he backed out. But when he whirled the wheel to make the turn and head downhill, the car slipped, the rear end coming around.

"Whoa." Benjamin couldn't stop his reaction.

"What? Worried?" Casey straightened the wheel and this time he took it a little slower. "Look at that. Clear path all the way down the hill."

The car handled just fine until they came to a curve. Ahead, they could see the intersection with a wider road, and Casey got a little too eager. The low-slung car didn't take the curve well, and the rear end swung around again. Casey over-corrected and before he could get it under control, the right rear tire took a sickening dip downward. Benjamin gripped a strap as he felt himself sinking to the lowest spot in the vehicle.

"Ditch!" Jacob called out, way too late to make a difference.

"No problem," Casey said, teeth clenched. "I'll just give it a little more—"

But more power wasn't the answer. The wheel spun and the whole right side of the car settled. No way were they getting out of here under their own power, Benjamin realized, shoving the ice chest off of him.

Casey let out a bunch of expletives, f-bombs flying all over the place. Jacob turned and reached between the seats for the cooler. "Miller time?"

Casey shoved his door open and got out, letting it slam behind him. The barrage of language still flew.

"Guess we'll have to crawl out of here," Benjamin told Jacob. "Looks like your door is wedged."

By the time they'd crawled over the console and out the driver's door, Casey had cooled off a little. "We'll need a tow truck. I'll call one when we get back to the cabin."

How? But Benjamin knew better than to say it out loud.

Lyle was practically laughing—okay, it was more like a smirk—when they came walking up to the front porch. "I got work to do." *Young fools.* He walked out to the barn, leaving them to stomp the snow off their boots.

Nancy met them at the door. "Well, boys, it doesn't look like this will be your day for snowboards," she said with a kindly smile. "But don't worry. There's plenty to do here and we'll keep ourselves busy."

Benjamin swore she sounded just like his mother, back when he was five. But the three guys followed her inside. Based on the scent coming from the kitchen, 'plenty to do' seemed to be baking cookies. Jacob got an eager look on his face.

Chapter 5

The days were getting longer already, Sam could tell. She woke before six and saw the faint tinge of light at the windows, a glow that wouldn't have been there a month ago. Beau's side of the bed was empty. No doubt he was already outside, tending to the ranch chores.

She brushed her teeth, pulled on jeans and a sweater, and reached for her jewelry box. After months at the center of a frightening situation, the ancient carved artifact had come back into everyday use, no longer banished to storage in the wall safe. And where once Sam had felt uncertain and even fearful of its powers, she now loved the old box. It held powers, and she might not fully understand them, but she'd come to accept it into her daily life.

She pulled out her favorite pair of gold hoop earrings, stroking the box's lumpy carved surface when she closed the lid. Predictably, the wood changed from a dark hue to a golden glow and warmed to her touch. Maybe it would give her some type of insight into the new case she and Kelly were now in the midst of.

Downstairs, she detected the scents of coffee and a residual of the toast Beau must have made for himself. The coffee maker was on warming mode and she poured herself a mug of the same blend she featured at Sweet's Sweets. The taste, and the sight of the bakery box she'd left on the countertop, reminded her that she'd not yet finalized any new designs for Easter and the holiday was sneaking up quickly. She would need to stop in at the bakery and spend some brainstorming time with the rest of the crew.

But first, she'd promised Kelly she would stop by early this morning. She transferred her coffee to a travel mug and headed out. With the last storm now four days behind them, the roads around town were clear.

Sam spotted an unfamiliar vehicle at the turnoff to Kelly and Scott's driveway, a pickup truck with a logo on the door. Gurule Excavations was printed on the side. Scott was standing there, speaking with the driver, when she came to a stop.

"What's up? You're not having the old house bulldozed, are you?" she teased. She knew better. Her son-in-law loved the Victorian home.

"Just planning to grade the driveway and lay down some new base course," he said. "Johnny says it's a little early for that. Need for the ground to completely thaw and the mud to dry up. But I wanted to get the estimate and be first on the list."

Sam recognized Johnny Gurule, whose father had done some dirt work at her previous home. Businesses tended to stay within families in this part of the world. He looked up from his clipboard and gave a little wave.

"Kelly's up and is chomping at the bit to fill you in on something she's learned," Scott said. "Ana spent the night with a friend. The parents are taking them to Meow Wolf in Santa Fe this morning."

Sam smiled and headed up the drive, avoiding the potholes and squishy ruts that inevitably formed on all dirt roads during the winter and spring months. Maybe she and Beau should take a closer look at their own driveway and parking area at the ranch.

She pulled under the portico outside the kitchen door and saw lights on inside.

"Hey there," Kelly said, carrying a skillet from the stove to the sink. "We just finished breakfast. Did you eat?"

"I'm fine." One of these days she intended to get serious about losing the extra twenty pounds—it might as well start now, while she was preoccupied with a mystery to solve and an upcoming holiday.

"So, I talked to Summer again last night and got some more info, as per Beau's instructions." Kelly dried her hands on a towel and tilted her head upward. "I've printed some pictures she sent me, and I have numbers for the parents of the other guys. Figured we could call them today?"

"Sounds good." Sam followed as Kelly led the way up the wide staircase to the second floor where they stopped at Scott's office in the turret room to pick up the images off his printer.

Kelly shuffled the pages as she walked toward the narrower stairway that led to the third floor attic room she'd claimed as her own space. The door was standing open and Eliza, the calico cat, lay sunning herself on the window seat.

"A set for you and a set for me," Kelly said, handing Sam some of the photos from her friend. "I can always print more if we have to give these away."

They pulled stools up to the heavy trestle table that served as workspace, experiment space, and all-around center of the room.

"Just to stay organized, I also typed out a list with the three young men's names, parents' names, their home addresses and phone numbers, and whatever else Summer told me. Obviously, the info on her brother Casey is the most complete. That's him," she said, pointing to two of the photos.

Casey Hardwick was tall and thin with dark eyes, sun-blonded hair, and a quirky, winning smile that told Sam he was probably an instigator, a ringleader, and a charmer with the girls. As Beau had predicted, one of the pictures was posed, probably for a yearbook. Another showed him leaning against a red Mustang—not exactly a new one, but not really vintage either. His weight was on one leg, with the other bent jauntily at the knee, toe on the ground, arms crossed, head tilted. A pair of expensive sunglasses sat atop his head, and she would have sworn he'd deliberately flexed his biceps just as the camera captured him.

Sam held out another of the pictures. "This is Casey, too, right?"

"Yeah. High school age, according to Summer. The other guy with him is Jacob Winters. They've been friends since fifth grade."

The second guy had the pale, pudgy look of a kid who spent most of his time at a video game console. He could be either super slow or super brilliant—it was impossible to tell from a picture.

"And we have this because Jacob is one of those who's now missing?"

"Right."

"But we don't have a photo of the third young man?"

"Not yet. Summer only knew his name is Benjamin Packard and Casey knows him from USC."

"That's where they all attend school?"

"Yep, at the Los Angeles campus. All live at home—well, in Casey's case, it's his sister's home. I got the impression Benjamin's parents are well-off and could get him into whatever school he wanted. The other two are on financial assistance, but apparently doing well enough scholastically to have made it into their third year."

Sam again studied the photo that included Jacob Winters. Must be higher on the super-brilliant scale than she'd first thought.

"I did a little digging and found Benjamin Packard's parents. Some distant relation to the Packard Bell dynasty ... or maybe that was Hewlett Packard ... or ... I don't know. That's just not my thing, Mom."

"Unless it's relevant to what we're doing now, I agree. Doesn't matter. The point is, this Benjamin comes from enough money that he could have gotten into any school he wanted—if I'm understanding the story."

"And if *I'm* understanding it. Summer didn't seem to be all that clear on it herself."

"But you said you have the parents' contact info? Let's just start calling around." Sam set the photos down on the table and picked up her phone. She tapped out the digits for Lisa Packard's phone and set it to be on speaker.

"You've reached the mobile number of Lisa Cummings Packard

and Home First Realty! Please leave me a message and I'll get right back!" The voice was perky and if Sam were in the market for a home in California, she would totally believe that Lisa would be right on it.

She left a message saying simply that she was calling from Taos, New Mexico, on the recommendation of Casey Hardwick's family. Surely, if Lisa was concerned about her own son, she'd quickly respond.

The number for Benjamin's father was answered by an automated system, stating she had reached Tech-to-the-Max. *Enter the extension for the party you wish to reach.* Not a lot of other options were given. Sam and Kelly exchanged a look and a shrug, and she clicked off the call.

"Hopefully, the mom calls back," Kelly said.

"The other kid's name is Jacob Winters—do we have his family's numbers?"

Kelly shuffled papers. "Yep, here somewhere. I can't believe how many little notes I made."

She'd planted her finger on one of the notes in a triumphant found-it move, when Sam's phone rang, showing Lisa Packard's number. She answered and put the call on speaker.

"Lisa Cummings Packard, returning your call."

Sam introduced herself and Kelly, and quickly explained how they'd come to have her number and that it was important for Casey's family to reach him.

"Casey Hardwick's sister is the one who contacted me," Kelly said. "First off, can you tell us if you've heard from your son since the three young men left on their spring break trip?"

"Well, no," Lisa said. "I mean, it's unusual. Benjie texts me pretty often but we're not, like, joined at the hip or anything. I'm *not* a helicopter mom."

"And all three of them are over twenty-one, aren't they?"

"Benjie hit that mark just before the school year started last fall. I think Casey and ... sorry, can't think of his name right now."

"Jacob Winters."

"Right. I think they're a year or so older."

"Did your son leave you with a copy of their itinerary, let you in on the plans?" Sam asked.

"I offered to use my real estate contacts to find them a rental place, but they wanted to do it on their own. Used some online site called 'Rent a Crib' or something like that. Hang on a sec. I think ..." Her voice went faint for a moment. "Yeah, I see it in my email. Benjie said he would forward it to me. Guess he did."

"Can you send that along to us?" Sam asked. "Or, if you'd be more comfortable about it, send it to the Taos County Sheriff's Department. Sheriff Evan Richards has also been contacted about this. We've often worked closely with the department." Which was technically true, although not in a while.

"Just give me an address," Lisa said. "Doesn't matter which."

Kelly's brow wrinkled but she recited Sam's email.

"One other favor," Sam asked. "If you hear from Benjamin, could you please let us know? Or let Summer Hardwick Gaines know. She's the one who really needs to reach her brother, and quickly."

"Um, sure. Sorry, I've got another call coming in and it's an offer on a million-dollar property. I need to take it. Feel free to reach out if there's anything else I can help you with." And she was gone.

"Well. Not exactly a picture of a doting, concerned mother, was she?" Sam said.

"Times have changed. There's no way you would have let me head off with friends for spring break, never check in, and give you little idea about where I went," Kelly said, tapping her pen against the tabletop.

"Good luck when Ana gets that age," Sam said with a grin.

"Oh no. We're home schooling her now. We'll just home school her right through college."

"Good thing you have a few years to relax a little first." She picked up her phone and swiped over to check emails. "Looks like Lisa did follow through on that anyway. The vacation rental site is called RentMyCrib.com. Catchy. The details are a little bit too tiny to read on a phone screen. Can we link my phone to Scott's printer and get hard copies?"

"I'm sure we can, if I can remember how. Or we can get the info from Evan."

Sam wished they had done that yesterday.

Chapter 6

When a woman answered at the Winters' home, they went through the same routine of introducing themselves and explaining the connection to Casey Hardwick's family. She readily identified herself as Bea, Jacob's mother.

"Oh, I *know*—I've been getting more and *more* worried by the day, ever since Summer called here." Bea's voice pegged her as a bit older, a lot more uncertain than the mom from their previous call.

"So, I take it that you've not heard from your son either?" Sam asked.

"My last call that got through to him, he said they were somewhere north of Albuquerque and driving toward Taos. That's where you said you're from? Well, anyway, the call got real staticky and we lost the connection. The mountains, I assumed. We'd left it that he would call again when he could. I suppose it's pretty wild country up there."

Not so wild that we don't have modern technology, Sam thought. But she didn't say so.

"I've tried calling Jacob's number multiple times a day, ever since then, and it always goes right to voicemail. I know he and Casey are together, and they've always looked out for each other, since they were ten years old, but there are the little things a mom worries about, you know. He didn't take a warm enough coat, and he left the snack bag behind, the one I'd packed for him."

Kelly sort of rolled her eyes toward Sam, and Sam sent her a look that said, *I wouldn't have been nearly this fussy about you.* What Benjamin's mother lacked in outward concern, Bea Winters made up in spades.

"I know, I'm a worrier," she said now, as though she'd read their thoughts. "But Jacob is my baby. I don't know if you have kids, but there's something about the youngest and the only boy. The girls grew up and got out on their own, just fine. But he's my late-in-life child, the only one still at home, and I just … Well, Stanley says I just can't let go of our son. And I know that. Stan's got his job at the post office—from which he'll retire in another few years—true. But for me, Jacob and my volunteer church work are my whole world."

"Casey's sister told me no one's heard from the boys for several days now. Had you notified law enforcement about that?" Sam asked.

"I've been in touch with Summer Hardwick—well, that's not her married name now. But anyway, she said she was calling the sheriff up there, so I let her take the lead on behalf of all of us."

"Good thinking. And yes, she did file a report. Did she tell you that the authorities weren't able to find out much at all?"

"Yes. And that's another thing—"

"Which you can certainly follow up on by calling Sheriff Evan Richards yourself. But I can tell you that we're working closely with him to share information too. It's why we're calling to get some basic information."

Kelly went into the questions they'd covered with the other families. Were the boys paying for the trip with a credit card—from a parent or one of their own? Bea said she didn't know. She hadn't given Jacob a card to use. Would they have driven straight through or stayed in a motel somewhere along the way?

"I'm sure they drove straight through. It's about fourteen hours, according to Jacob, and Casey trusted him to take turns with the driving, even though Casey loves that Mustang car about as much as he loves anything in the world."

"I wonder if they checked the weather reports ahead of time?" Sam asked.

An audible sigh. "I doubt it. Of the three boys, Benjamin was the type to think of stuff like that. Jacob would be sure there was food in the car. Casey would just jump in behind the wheel and start out."

"We can check on that," Kelly said. "Although you said you did speak with your son while they were on the road somewhere north of Albuquerque, right?"

"Yes, I don't remember the name of the little town he said they were passing through."

They'd pretty well run out of questions for the moment, but Sam asked Bea to get in touch if she thought of anything else. "And most definitely call us if you hear directly from the boys."

"Oh, I sure will. It's a big relief to me to know someone in New Mexico is actually looking for them now. I can't tell you how worried—"

"For sure. We will keep you updated as we learn anything new." Kelly was rolling her hand, signaling to Sam that they should wrap this up.

They ended the call after another round of assurances.

"I could see that going on another hour without covering any new ground," Kelly said.

"She's just—"

"Worried. It shows."

"Let's take a look back at the weather for the date they were supposed to arrive," Kelly said, "and I'll go check Scott's printer to see if we got that receipt to print."

No luck on the receipt but Kelly spotted Scott, on his way up the driveway. "He'll figure it out."

Sam had gotten to a weather app on her phone and backtracked the reports to March 26 and 27, when the trio was due to arrive at Taos Ski Valley.

"Looks like that was the evening we had all that wind," she said. "I remember there being four or five inches of snow, and it wasn't too bad, but the wind really drifted it around. Beau and I didn't have any problem getting out of our driveway with our pickup trucks, but I can't imagine a low sports car would have managed it very well. And the ski valley would have received more snow than we got around town."

She turned to see that Kelly had walked out of the attic room, and now she could hear voices on the level below, Kelly explaining to Scott about the document they needed to print from Sam's phone.

"Have her forward the email and the attachment to my account. That's the quickest way," he was saying.

"Heard that. Got it." Sam tapped the necessary links and sent the message on its way.

She stood up and stretched, realizing she'd been sitting on the same wooden stool for more than an hour. On a shelf against the west wall, she spotted Kelly's carved wooden box—the mate to her own—and a familiar leather-bound book. They called it the book of runes because that's what the writing resembled, some ancient language of symbols. But both had discovered that after handling the wooden boxes they could read the words in the book perfectly. She pulled it from the shelf and carried it to the table.

Kelly walked in, carrying a sheet of paper. "Success! Looks like the RentMyCrib receipt is a simple one and the directions to the property are really basic."

She spotted the book on the table, where Sam had opened the cover and was running her thumbnail across the leaves of the pages.

"You think …?"

Sam shrugged. "I don't know. But I didn't get any strong clues from the phone conversations just now. And I did handle the box this morning."

Kelly set the receipt on the table and took the wooden artifact from the shelf, holding it close to her body, wrapping her forearms around it. As with the other one, the wood began to glow and warm her. When the box had become bright, golden, she set it down and stood beside Sam and the magic book.

"Shall we look for a topic or just go random?" Sam asked.

"You know how that goes." They'd long ago discovered that the book had no index or table of contents. In fact, no discernable method of organization at all. "Random it is."

Sam placed the spine on the table, her hands flat against the covers, and let the book fall open to an arbitrary page. They both stared at the image on the antique parchment sheet.

Kelly reached for the receipt she'd carried from the printer. "Um, listen to the description of the property those college kids rented. 'Your fairytale cottage awaits your arrival. Complete with all amenities, you'll feel as though you are spending your vacation in an enchanted forest.'" She looked up. "Mom, this is just plain weird."

The watercolor artwork in the book depicted a cottage with gingerbread trim, spiral-carved porch posts, mounded snow on the shingles, and perfect icicles dripping from the roofline. Surrounding it was a dense pine forest of snow-covered trees. A narrow track led to the porch, with three small sets of footprints visible in the snow.

"As in, Hansel and Gretel weird."

"We'd better hope that the property owner isn't some kind of evil witch."

Sam felt a ripple of goosebumps travel up her arms as Kelly closed the book.

Chapter 7

Mother and daughter stared into each other's eyes for a long moment. Finally, Sam broke the silence. "Well, we've got the same directions the boys were given. I'd say we have to go check it out. Maybe Evan didn't go to the right house."

She read through the instructions carefully. "I know this area. Back in the day, there were a couple of houses I had to break into up there. I'm sure we can find it, although I have a feeling the 'charming cottage' aspect may have been overrated. Most of what I saw were just ordinary mountain cabins." She picked up her jacket and pulled it on. "We'll see."

Twenty minutes later, Sam was driving up Highway 150 and passing the improbably named Ocean Blvd. "We need to go on past the parking area and ski lift before we get into the area where most of the homes are."

"I got this, Mom. I programmed the address into my phone. Looks like we stay on this road for another quarter mile or so and then take a right."

"So, the address shows up? I wonder why three college-age young men didn't do the same thing you've done."

"They're men. Wouldn't that be the equivalent of asking for directions?"

Sam laughed. "Probably."

"I mean, seriously. The way Summer describes Casey. Confident—well, she said know-it-all—the kind of guy who never questions himself or shows uncertainty. I can *so* see him hopping in the car in California and telling his friends that he'd figure it out when he got here."

"Still … not one of them tried to double-check him?"

"Well, you know how electronics work, especially way back here where mountains are twelve, thirteen thousand feet all around you. There's only one or two cell carriers that have invested in the equipment to serve what's really a limited client base. Odds are pretty good that the guys didn't know that their provider didn't put a tower up here. They may have learned it the hard way."

"Right. We locals buy what we know will work here. People from big cities don't give it a second thought. I see it in the bakery all the time, customers who need to use our wi-fi because they aren't getting a signal."

"Okay, there's your left turn," Kelly said, pointing. "And then it's a quick right. Once we've done that, it should be the second cabin on the right."

And there it was, complete with gingerbread trim and spiral porch posts.

"This is eerie." Kelly stared at the single set of car

tracks that led up the inclined driveway, made a turn, and left again. "The book is eerie."

"Do we suppose the set of car tracks belongs to Casey and his friends?"

"I really doubt it. Maybe Evan's?"

"True. There was snow night before last. The tracks could be even more recent." Sam turned to Kelly. "Shall we test our luck and see if either of us has a phone signal? We need to talk to the cabin's owner."

"Hm, maybe I should have thought of that before we left home?"

"Doesn't matter. Try it now." Sam picked up the reservation receipt from her truck's console and read the phone number off to Kelly.

"It's ringing!" Kelly held absolutely still. As she had learned, even turning your head could lose an iffy signal here in the mountains.

When a female voice answered, she put the phone on speaker and went into the explanation about how they were trying to locate renters who would have been at the cabin.

"I'm aware," said the woman, who sounded forty-ish. "The local police called me first, and I'll tell you the same thing I told them. I rented the cabin online, got paid by credit card. I don't even keep the card info because all of that is handled by a payment service. Once I get paid, I email instructions. I live in Oklahoma and never even see my renters. It's a fairly easy way to earn enough to pay the expenses of the cabin property, although I can't say I'm earning much more than break-even."

"But the renters have someone local they can contact if there's a problem, don't they?"

"Sure. Inside the house is a list. I've got a maintenance

guy who can be called if, for instance, the heater quits or there's no water … that kind of thing. Name's Mitch—he's good and he's reliable. And a cleaner comes after each renter, does the linens and dishes. She also comes the day before any new renters arrive and makes sure everything is spotless and sanitized."

"The sheriff seemed unsure about whether either of those people saw this particular group."

"I checked with both of them, after his call. Maintenance guy never heard a word, which is good news to him and to me. I asked the cleaning woman, and that was the really weird part. She went up after I called, and she said there was no sign they'd ever been there. I mean, some of the renters leave the place in good shape, but this was more like untouched. No trash, no used dishes, no wrinkles in the sheets or towels. They never got there."

The cleaner's visit explained the tracks here now. Sam got that same chill up her arms.

Kelly thought of another question. "So, did they contact you and ask for their money back or anything like that?"

"Nope. The rental agreement is pretty specific. No refunds for late arrival or early departure. You pay in advance and that's that."

"Would you mind if we walked around the outside of the place, just taking a look to see if there's any sign of them?"

"Knock yourself out. If you need to go in, I could authorize Mitch to meet you there with a key."

"I don't see any need. If your cleaning service saw no sign they'd been into the cabin, we wouldn't find anything either."

"Sure. Good luck with it. I imagine it's a scary situation for any family, if they don't know where their kids went. Sorry I couldn't help you."

They ended the call and Sam looked toward Kelly. "Want to do that? Walk around the perimeter?"

She eyed the snow, especially at the sides of the cabin, where no plow had touched the ground all winter.

"I know. Me either."

"What about neighbors? Evan said the cabins are spaced kind of far apart out here, but I can kind of see one through the trees there. And I imagine sounds carry quite a ways. If anyone was home on either side of this one, they could have easily heard the vehicle, their voices …"

Sam put the truck in gear and backed out. A dark blue Suburban sat in the driveway of the cabin to the north, so they started with that place, pulling in behind it. Two children in bright snowsuits stopped their snowman project and stared. A woman of about thirty, wearing a plush pullover and her hair up in a messy bun, stepped out to the porch. She confirmed that her family owned the place but said they'd only arrived the night before, their first chance to get to the mountains since Christmas.

Kelly thanked her and they turned around, planning to check the other adjoining property. One glance told them not to bother. From the road they could tell the rustic cabin was closed up tight with wooden shutters over the windows and large drifts of snow across the driveway and front porch. No one had been there in months.

"What about the ski lift?" Kelly suggested. "They'd have to buy tickets. Maybe they have to show ID or something."

It seemed like a longshot but Sam was willing to follow

any breadcrumb at this point. They pulled into the nearly empty parking lot and made their way to the ticket window. A bored-looking scrawny guy with a wispy chin-beard looked up after Kelly cleared her throat to get his attention.

Sam went into the explanation that they were working with the sheriff's department to locate some missing men who may have bought lift tickets sometime around March 26 and 28. She needed some verification as to whether they'd been here. The attendant gave her a glazed look, until she suggested she could just have the sheriff come out and request the information himself.

She was about to try to get Evan on the phone when a woman walked into the booth through a back door. The embroidered name on her jacket identified her as the manager. Sam got her attention and went through her spiel again.

"No, we don't require ID in order to buy a lift ticket," the manager told her. "But, we do make people sign a liability release form. You know, it protects the ski area from a lawsuit if some bozo takes off for the out-of-bounds areas and then kills himself."

"You must have those releases on file here then?"

"You a lawyer? Got a warrant?"

Sam shook her head, repeated the part about how she was working with Sheriff Richards to help these families, and assured the woman her request was simply based on finding some proof that the three had actually made it to Taos Ski Valley at all. "If your kid took off for spring break somewhere far from home—maybe Florida or Mexico—wouldn't you be desperate to find out why you can't reach him now?"

That did the trick. "I can't just hand over all the records, you understand. Besides, all the paperwork is electronic these days. But if you'll leave me the three names I'll go through and search for them. I'll call you."

It was the best they were going to get. Sam wrote down the info, including both their phone numbers and that of Evan's direct line. She thanked the woman and added another plea for the families, but she still had the feeling that the search would be perfunctory at best.

Chapter 8

Why do I feel like we've just arrived at a dead end?" Kelly said as they walked back to Sam's truck.

"I know. Frustrating. Not much choice but to wait for an answer and see if any other ideas come to us. Meanwhile, we've both got our own things to handle." She climbed in the truck and started the engine.

Kelly glanced at the dashboard clock. "Yikes, it's getting close to noon. I'd better let Riki know I'm running late for work."

The parking lot outside both Puppy Chic and the bakery was bustling when they arrived fifteen minutes later. Sam pulled around to the alley that ran behind the businesses and Kelly hopped out. She'd cut back on her hours here after Ana was born, but still loved working with the dog groomer. The half-days, three times a week, helped

Riki Richards manage a busy schedule and gave Kelly a few hours outside the home.

Plus, Sam liked having her daughter right next door, for their impromptu little coffee breaks and the times Ana came along to help in the bakery. She gathered her phone and messenger bag and walked in the back door at Sweet's Sweets.

At first glance, it appeared that chaos reigned. Julio had both hands full with hot trays—one of croissants, one of muffins—which he deftly slid into the cooling racks beside the big bake oven. In his work area, the huge Hobart mixer was churning away, filled with what appeared to be a large batch of chocolate cake batter. He tossed down his oven mitts and eyed the progress of the batter.

"Seventeen sheet cakes," Becky explained when she noticed Sam eyeing the quantity. "Both of the elementary schools and the high school planned their Spring Fling parent/student events for the same day."

"How can I help?" Sam asked, shedding her bag and jacket and heading for the sink to wash up.

"At the moment, we're cool." Becky was piping buttercream roses onto waxed paper squares, setting each one on a flat baking sheet to set up. "These are for a quinceañera party later this afternoon. Julio's about to put the sheet cakes into the oven. They'll cool overnight, and tomorrow I'll whip out the decorations as quickly as possible. If you're going to be around, it'll go faster …"

"I'll plan on it."

"Luckily, Jen talked the parent-committee woman into doing the same design for all the elementary school cakes. We're going with a spring theme, which should be pretty quick to put together. Half the cakes are chocolate, half vanilla. Very basic. Just lots of them." She carried the tray of roses over to the walk-in fridge.

"Sounds like the lunch rush is in full swing," Sam said, tuning an ear toward the curtain that divided the kitchen from the sales room.

"Oh! I totally forgot. Your friend Rupert is here. He was back here in the kitchen, demolishing our supply of coconut balls, so I suggested he go try the spinach-mushroom-feta quiche. He's probably at one of the tables out front."

"Hm, we haven't seen much of Rupert in recent weeks," Sam said. "I guess I'd better talk to him. See what's he's been up to. Unless you need me back here for the next few minutes?"

"Nope. I'm finishing up these Easter bunny cupcakes for the display case, then I'm back to that quinceañera cake. After that … I'm not sure."

"I'll be back before you've finished all that," Sam promised. She picked up her favorite coffee mug from her desk, rinsed it, and walked out to the showroom.

As predicted, Rupert sat at one of the bistro tables, an empty plate in front of him and the local newspaper spread out over the table. His collar-length gray hair was combed back, but seemed limp today. Most notably, he wore gray and black—soft pants and a blousy tunic—with not a trace of his usual purple. Not a scarf nor an earring nor a pair of vivid purple slip-on shoes. His post-Christmas funk was apparently still on.

"Want some company?" Sam asked.

"Sammy! Girl, how are you?" He rose to his full six feet and brought her into an embrace. "You look well."

"I am. As are Kelly, Ana, Scott, and Beau. Whole family

is thriving." She filled her mug with hot water and chose an herbal teabag from the selection at the beverage bar, then joined him at the table.

"Kelly's husband is still writing his children's mystery series?"

Sam nodded. "From what I can tell, it's going gangbusters. He always seems to be on a deadline for the next one."

Rupert folded his newspaper and sighed. "Me too, and I am so blocked."

Under the pen name of Victoria DeVane, he wrote steamy romances that never failed to hit the top of the charts.

"So … what's the deal? No plot ideas?"

"No inspiration. Mark. I'm not getting over him."

Sam didn't know what to say. Rupert and Mark had vacationed in the tropics during the holidays and the romance looked to be on a trajectory toward permanence. Then all at once, Mark was gone and Rupert was wearing dreary colors.

"Maybe you need to talk to someone? Figure some way to work it out?"

"He was The One, Sam. I had rings. I proposed on the beach under a full moon. How much more romantic does it get?"

She watched as he stared into his macchiato.

"He said no. Just flat out no. Couldn't commit." A long sigh. "And after that, nothing's the same. We barely talked during the final week of the vacation, and then he left for Austin when we got back. Said he had to get back into expressing himself, and the music scene was the place for him."

Sam reached out and squeezed his hand. "I wish I knew what advice to give. It's got to be a challenge to write a romance after a break up like that."

"More like impossible. I can't even think."

"What if you took the strongest emotion you're coping with right now and turned that into the central plot element? What are you feeling—sadness, anger, betrayal, abandonment?" Sam checked her thoughts. Where had all that come from? She knew nothing about writing a book.

But Rupert seemed to have latched onto it. "And *use* that emotion! Use it in some way, either for or against my characters." He was staring across the room, but not eyeing the pastries with the same hunger with which he'd consumed eight coconut balls earlier.

"And maybe if you built this story into something beyond purely a romance. Added some mystery or elements of a thriller … I don't know."

"Not sure what my editor would say, but at this point she'd probably take anything that runs seventy-thousand words and has Victoria's name on it." He drummed his fingers on the table. "Okay, now for a mystery or thriller thread. Any ideas on that?"

Sam gave a fond smile. "Actually, I do. Three kids take off for spring break, don't show at their destination, and no one's heard a word. Where did they really go and what happened to them?"

"This is real, isn't it?"

"Yeah, actually." She filled him in on the basics.

"I know a woman with a house up there, quite a showplace. She inherited something like two bazillion shares of Amazon stock and just lets it support her while she sits out on her deck and watches the ski valley activity all day. You could talk to her, see if she saw these kids."

He pulled out his phone and made the call, but of course it went straight to voicemail and he ended up leaving a message.

"So, she knows I'll be calling at some point. It's worth a try anyway. Thanks, Rupe. Did any of this give you a story idea?"

"Maybe something historical. Instead of spring break, these young men head out on some kind of Western adventure. Did you know, at one time, there really was a serial killer with a cabin who lured people in and they were never seen again? It was over the other side the mountain from here, Moreno Valley."

Sam was shaking her head. "Sounds tragic to me."

"His Indian wife escaped one night while he was drunk, and she made it to a town up the road. Told the townspeople what he was doing. A lynch mob went after the guy."

"Sounds *really* tragic to me."

"Okay, okay—probably so." He was typing something on his phone. "Remember that movie some years back, where Demi Moore and Chevy Chase are this couple who lose their way and end up in an old guy's junkyard? It was scary and yet hilarious at the same time."

Sam did remember the movie and she smiled. But still … "I'm not sure Victoria DeVane is really known for hilarious or scary, but you'll have fun playing around with ideas until you hit the right note."

"Yeah," he said with a sigh. His brief moment of enthusiasm flickered out.

Sam finished her tea and found her attention drawn to the bakery's front display window. A couple of weeks ago, she'd hastily assembled some standard Easter designs—eggs and chicks and bunnies, all recreated with durable plastic and foam, decorated with royal icing, which wouldn't melt in the heat from the sunny window.

But it was nothing spectacular, and now, with just a few days to go, she wanted to spark it up with something that would draw people to the window and into the bakery to order their own. What would it be?

Her mind's eye immediately took her to the magic book in Kelly's attic and the image on the page she had randomly opened it to. She could do something with that. But was she using someone else's tragedy to swipe creative ideas, or was she putting it out to the universe that this was a situation that needed answers?

Chapter 9

"Honey, where did you go last night? You came in late. I heard the truck." Nancy snuggled into Lyle's shoulder, not meeting his eyes.

He didn't answer. Dawn lit the horizon outside their bedroom window. Nearly time to get up, make breakfast. She likely wouldn't have another chance to talk privately for the rest of the day.

"Lyle?"

"Had to get rid of that car."

"What?"

"They're gov'ment, those boys."

She raised up on one elbow, staring at her husband. "What on earth are you saying? How do you know any of that?"

"The car. Got California plates—"

"They *told* us they're from California. That's not suspicious." Except maybe in Lyle's book.

"Don't interrupt me," he hissed. "California plates and a window sticker for parking at the Braxton Lab. They do top secret stuff there, develop ways to spy on ordinary people. Probably know too much about us already. Them types can trick you into saying stuff you don't want to."

Nancy fell back against her pillow. "Oh, Lyle. This is really getting—" She closed her mouth. There was no getting through to him when he started on about the conspiracy theories he read about in those magazines of his.

Wouldn't it have been simpler to just pull the car out of the ditch, load the boys up in it, and send them on down the road? What was he thinking? The joke had gone too far. It was one thing to trick three kids into staying for a few days during the storm and while their vehicle was stuck, but this couldn't lead to anything good. She would have to let her husband cool off again, then get him alone and talk some sense to him. She would make his favorite breakfast, waffles and bacon.

The toilet flushed in the other bathroom. Nancy rushed to get dressed before the boys began wandering through the house. She'd managed to keep them busy during three stormy days with the video games in the rec room—and she had to admit she was regaining her old skills with Pac Man in the process—but she sensed their restlessness. Today, they would want out. Why couldn't Lyle have simply let that happen?

She bustled into the kitchen and scooped coffee into the basket of her old-fashioned percolator. She gave it a wry grin as she plugged it in. One of these days it would give out and she'd be forced to unbox the Mr. Coffee that sat on the top pantry shelf, the one Cindy had given her for Mother's Day, what … twenty years ago? Could it possibly have been that long since their daughter announced her departure by calling her dad a 'crazy paranoid old coot'?

Nancy still received a birthday card and a Mother's Day card each year, postmarked from different cities in the beginning, coming from Boston these past ten or more years. There was rarely a call, never a letter, and Nancy understood why. Anything written down could be intercepted, calls could be monitored. She shook her head and wondered when Lyle-the-adventurous had become Lyle-the-nutcase. Maybe if they'd had more children, sons. But she reminded herself, as she often did, that scenario could mean she'd be living with three or four paranoid men, not just the one.

A sound at the kitchen door caught her attention, and she looked up into the glass door of the microwave, checking her expression and arranging her features into a benign and friendly mask.

"Good morning, Benjamin," she said. "Coffee will be ready in a jiff. And I was thinking of waffles for breakfast, but I can cook you some eggs if you'd like."

"Anything's fine. Don't go to any extra trouble."

That was Benjamin, she decided. The wispy one with his sandy brown hair and green eyes, younger than the others in more ways than years. Quiet, probably good in school because he had that studious look about him. The kind of son she would have liked because they would spend hours doing things together—reading, watching the wildlife and looking up each new critter that wandered through the property, studying things like the planets and stars. An agreeable kid who just as readily accepted that with no internet he could be content to play old games and watch VHS movies. Lyle would like this kid because he was open to ideas and wouldn't argue back.

The others, not so much. Jacob spent the day rummaging for snacks and stuffing his face. His unfit physique would irritate Lyle, and the older man would be lecturing him constantly. And Casey—that one was a ringleader, a girl-catcher, and a pretty shallow personality. He and Lyle would butt heads. They already had. Which reminded Nancy about this morning's conversation. Her stomach tensed.

The percolator stopped bubbling. "Coffee's ready," she announced, fetching a mug for Benjamin and one for Lyle, who would walk in at any minute.

She filled one of the mugs, handed it across the counter and gestured for Benjamin to take a seat and help himself to sugar and cream. She remembered he took both. Pulling out her large mixing bowl, she assembled the ingredients—flour, milk, eggs, vanilla—set the waffle iron on the counter and plugged it in to preheat.

"Wow, you make waffles from scratch?" Benjamin watched in fascination as she cracked two eggs into the bowl. "When I was little my mom would use a mix from a box. Now she just keeps some in the freezer and I stick 'em in the toaster when I want one."

"This isn't hard to do. I could teach you."

He gave a smile (a wistful one, she imagined). "I don't think we even have all those ingredients in the house most of the time."

"So, your mom works at something that keeps her pretty busy?"

"Real estate. She's good at it. Every time she does a closing, she treats herself to a weekend at some really fancy spa place. It's pretty often."

"And your dad?"

"Oh, he's brilliant—well, I guess. He pulls down big bucks at Ganymede Tech—in the Tech-to-the-Max division—as a programmer. Sometimes, when they're working on a really big coding project, he's up all night working out the details. But that's more recent stuff. When I was little, he was our Scoutmaster and we went camping and hiking and all that. He could start a campfire with a couple of sticks and a rock."

"Impressive." She whisked flour into the batter mixture until the consistency was right. "What about brothers and sisters?"

"Nope. Just me." He held the coffee mug with both hands, warming them.

"What are you studying in school? All of you guys are in college, right?"

"Yeah, I'm majoring in web development, with an eye toward—"

Lyle walked into the kitchen and eyed the progress on the waffle batter. "Coffee?"

Nancy handed him the mug she'd just filled. "Benjamin was just telling me about school."

Lyle grunted and didn't ask for details. His eyes flicked toward the dining room and the doorway that led to the entryway. Casey had opened the front door, shrugging into his jacket as he stepped outside.

Nancy subconsciously followed the moves, and the mood. A twinge shot through her stomach.

It didn't take two minutes before Casey stormed back inside, throwing the front door open, cursing like a sailor.

"Where's my damn car!" A dozen f-bombs followed as his heavy footsteps reverberated.

Nancy set down her package of bacon, Benjamin hunched a little closer to the breakfast bar. Lyle squared his narrow shoulders and raised his chin defiantly. Almost in slow motion he set his mug down and walked toward the stormy young man.

"My car's gone."

"Did it ever occur to you that someone might have pulled it out of the ditch as a favor?"

"Did you?"

"Not me. Maybe the police came along, saw it there, towed it."

Casey didn't believe a word of it. Nancy gritted her teeth. What was Lyle doing?

They were a picture. The seventy-six year old man, built like a wire whip, facing down the taller, broad-shouldered college kid. Logic said the larger guy could easily take down the smaller, older one. But there was something in the air … something dangerous. Casey sensed it and backed down, out of steam.

"I need to call somebody, find out where they took it," he said, not quite meeting Lyle's hard eyes.

Lyle didn't budge.

Benjamin tapped his phone screen to wake it and reaffirm that there was no signal, still.

"Try the phone in the living room." Nancy was surprised to hear her voice come out without a waver.

Casey fired one last glare toward Lyle as he spun on his heel and left the room. A moment later—"Shit!"

Nancy watched her husband as he picked up his coffee again, a small smile on his face.

Chapter 10

Sam tamped down a mounting sense of doom as she slogged through waist-deep snow, looking for someone who would talk with her. Trees blocked her view of anything ahead and she felt as though she'd been trekking for hours and going nowhere. The cabin she *knew* was just beyond the next tree never showed up. The snow kept getting deeper and her legs wouldn't move.

Then something touched her shoulder.

"Sam. Sam, wake up!"

Her eyes opened slowly and saw Beau leaning over her. *Oh, thank God.*

"Honey, you were thrashing around. You've got the sheets all tangled."

No wonder her legs weren't working. She let her body go limp, willed the tension to go away.

"That must have been some dream," he said, stroking her shoulder.

"Ugh. One of those frustrating ones where you have a goal and never quite find it. It had something to do with our search for those young men, but other than being trapped in a big snowdrift, I can't figure out how it's supposed to tie together."

"So, no answers."

"None at all. What time is it?" She rolled toward the bedside clock. 4:19.

"Still dark out. Come over here." His tone conveyed the mood exactly, and while she wasn't exactly feeling sexy right now, she knew if she followed his lead, it would most certainly take her mind off the subject that had dominated her dreams.

She rolled over and let the next thirty minutes work Beau's spell on her.

An hour later, she was dressed and feeling energized enough to get an early start at the bakery. Beau had taken a record-time shower and was already in the kitchen when she went downstairs, a travel mug of coffee ready for her. Ranger and Nellie were wolfing down their breakfast, and she gave each dog a scratch behind the ears.

"As much as I'd like to think you'd want to hang out in bed together all day, I know better," he said, placing a gentle kiss on her forehead.

"Much as I would *love* to do that … you know how every upcoming holiday stacks up the work at the bakery. Becky has a bunch of sheet cakes to finish this morning, and that doesn't even touch the other orders or the window display."

He gave a little sideways grin. "Makes me fairly glad I

have no clue how to decorate a cake. I have a feeling I'd be recruited."

"You handle horses, I'll handle cakes." She moved to the front door, pulled her coat on, and kissed him properly before taking the mug from him.

"See you when I see you," he said, maybe a little wistfully.

Sam let the sexy morning awakening settle over her, leaving her mind a blank canvas for ideas as she headed into town. The alley behind the bakery was empty and she knew she would have the place to herself for a little while until Julio came to begin the morning pastries.

All evening her mind had buzzed with ideas for transforming the enchanting cottage from the picture in the book, into something that would now entice more customers into her shop. The real cabin in the woods had looked uncannily similar to the picture. Was she tempting fate or playing with reality too much?

She debated the question as she flipped on kitchen lights, preheated the oven, and put coffee on to brew at the beverage bar. Yesterday's experiences had coalesced in her brain in one positive way. She had what she thought was a brilliant idea for the window display, so she cleared one end of the work table and began pulling out ingredients for gingerbread.

During the Christmas season, Sam baked so many gingerbread houses she had a pattern ingrained into her mind. Now, she followed the lines from memory and cut panels to form the walls and roofs of two structures. One would be a house, the other a small chapel.

While the pieces baked, she sipped her freshened coffee and reached for her messenger bag, where she had stashed the wooden box. Today she would need creativity and energy, in equal measures. She only hoped the box would work its usual magic. She closed her eyes and let images come to her.

The timer told her to take the crisp gingerbread pieces from the oven, and while they cooled, Sam got busy with royal icing, color gel, and pastry bags. Her hands flew as tulips, daffodils, and hyacinths appeared almost effortlessly. She set the flowers aside to dry and picked up the boards she normally used as a base for her window displays. She covered two of them in fresh parchment paper and began assembly on the cottage first. As her mind envisioned the drawing from the book yesterday, the reality came together in cookie panels. Rather than a wintery, snowy effect, this time every decoration was in springtime tones.

At some point Julio arrived and said, "Cute." He'd always been a man of few words.

While he proceeded to mix batter for the various quick breads and muffins that comprised their standard breakfast fare, Sam set the landscape pieces in place around the cottage. Tall pine trees, water-colored and attached to cardboard, were the only inedible elements. She didn't often do it that way, priding herself on making every aspect of a custom dessert something that could be pulled off and eaten. But she'd gotten a late start this year and now time was of the essence.

A carpet of spring flowers filled the grassy lawn she had created around the structure, and in a moment of real inspiration, she piped the shapes of animals—deer, bunnies, a pair of raccoons—and a couple dozen birds. While those dried enough to be handled, she began on the second building, the chapel, which she set up on the opposite side of the clearing from the cottage.

The flowers around the chapel would be lilies, of course, and she would let the daffodils and tulips spread their bright color there, as well. She stood back to assess the work just as the back door opened and Becky walked in.

"Oh! Sam, that is *amazing*. My kids would call it awesome—and I have to agree." She circled the tableau, taking in the details.

"Still a few details to add," Sam said, showing her the royal icing figures of the birds and animals. "Want to pick up those tweezers and help me set them in place?"

The two of them went to work.

"You know, the only shame about these fantastic window displays is that they can't be kept until next year. Once the holiday is over, we just end up taking them home for the kids to eat. And, I tell you, mine don't need any more sugar after their Easter baskets are gone."

An idea flashed into Sam's head. "What if … I mean, the spring season lasts well beyond Easter Sunday … So, maybe we could …"

Becky stood with eyebrows raised, paused with a little frosting fawn sitting delicately on her hand.

"How about if we give them away? Hold a drawing or contest?"

"I love it! We'll put a sign in the front window that says 'Win this scene' or something like that. People who come in can fill out a little entry slip."

"And the Saturday before Easter we hold a drawing and they can take the whole thing home."

"It's pretty big," Becky reminded.

"Two buildings, two winners," Julio said from his side

of the kitchen. Who knew he'd even been listening?

"Great idea! We'll draw separately for the cottage and for the chapel and two people can each take something home. Good thing I set them up on two separate boards."

They once again stepped back to look over the work, put a finishing touch here and there.

"They're fairly heavy," Sam reminded. "Julio, maybe you can help me set them in place?"

Becky dusted sugar off her hands. "Well, there's no shortage of things to work on the rest of the morning. Remember the seventeen sheet cakes for this afternoon at the schools."

"Have we decided how they'll be decorated?" Sam asked.

"There are so many, I'm thinking fairly simple. Maybe we could incorporate each school's colors to make them stand out a little?"

Sam surveyed the crowded worktable, where there was absolutely no space left for that many cakes. She watched as Julio removed two big tins of muffins from the oven, then the two of them carried the cottage scene to the sales room.

She quickly moved the previous display, a four-tier wedding cake topped with spring flowers and draped with folds of fondant, and set it on one of the bistro tables. She could reset things in the second display window to accommodate it. And a few of the lesser items could be discarded. Better to keep the presentation fresh.

With the cottage tucked neatly on the righthand side of the space, they went back for the chapel. Once it was in place on the left, Sam brought more of the painted pine trees and set them up to create the idyllic setting of two charming buildings in the forest. She walked out the front door to stand in front of the shop and view the result.

"When did you put this together?" Jen asked, getting out of her car and walking up.

"I woke up super early, didn't have anything else to do." Sam nearly blushed, remembering how she and Beau had spent some time, after she'd come out of her confusing dreams.

They walked back inside and Jen flipped over the Open sign and turned on the overhead lights. Donning her company apron, she surveyed the nearly empty display case.

"Julio's got a bunch more ready in the kitchen. I kind of distracted him with setting up the window," Sam told her. "We'll get this full in no time."

Two cars had already pulled up outside.

Sam filled in Jen on the idea for the drawing as they walked to the kitchen together.

"What a great idea. I can make a couple of signs for the window, and maybe we can create some little slips for names and phone numbers and print them on your computer?"

Somewhere in her spare time, Sam thought, as she saw Becky loading the worktable with sheet cakes. She also needed to get with Kelly at some point to see if the ski operators had found those three young guys' names in their records, and she should check in with Evan Richards. Maybe his department was having better luck in the search than she and Kelly had.

She took a breath and lifted a tray of croissants that were still warm and so fragrant. Jen had muffins, while Julio carried two—cinnamon rolls and filled Danish. In no time, the cases were full, and the first customers through the door were already remarking on the beautiful window display.

Jen found a pad of notepaper and told them about the contest, asking them to write down their names and numbers if they wanted to enter. And Sam went back to put her Spring Fling decorating ideas to the test on those cakes.

Chapter 11

It was a little after noon when Kelly popped in at Sweet's Sweets. "Holy cow! Did an Easter basket explode in here?" She was eyeing the array of sheet cakes, which now boasted basketweave trim, piped sprigs of icing 'grass' and an array of jellybeans and malted milk eggs, artfully arranged so every slice of each cake would be a generous one.

"Much as I wanted to create something artful, we had to admit these are for schoolkids who aren't going to appreciate the art. It's a Spring Fling. Let them live it up a little, right?"

"We'll let their parents deal with the sugar high after school." Becky gave a little grin as she set the first of the cakes into one of their purple bakery boxes.

"Here, let me help with that," Kelly offered. She hung

up her sweater and began assembling more boxes.

Sam applied her logo sticker to each box and carried them, two at a time, to the sales room where they would await the customers who were coming to pick them up.

"I need to call Summer again," Kelly said. "At least fill her in on what we've done so far. She could be thinking we aren't even working on it."

"I'm surprised none of the families have come out here to do their own investigating."

"Well, we know Summer's situation. She's pretty much tied to her dying mother's bedside. And I got the feeling the Packards are such a power couple in their careers, they just trust that their kid is fending for himself—probably because at home that's what he does."

Sam nodded. "Jacob's mother seemed worried enough. She wouldn't pick up and come?"

Kelly shrugged. "I suppose it would be a good idea for us to reach out again. Maybe one of them has heard from their son and just didn't bother to let us know."

"True." Sam picked up the final cake box. When she returned to the kitchen, Kelly was on the phone with Summer, her voice raised slightly to be heard over the clatter of pans and the motor on the Hobart.

"I should have probably gone out to my car for a phone conversation," she told Sam after she'd hung up.

"Any word?"

"Unfortunately not. The good news is that her mom is still hanging in there. I got the feeling she expects to see Casey any day now. But I didn't give any false hope about the chances of our locating him. I told her we hadn't yet found a solid lead of any kind."

Sam reached into her bag for the notebook she'd begun

keeping, what she thought of as her case file. She'd written down the phone numbers for all the families along with a few notes about the conversations.

"No one but Jen is out front right now. We could make calls there."

"Good idea," Kelly said. "And I want a honey bran muffin."

While she helped herself to the pastry and poured a fresh mug of coffee, Sam sat at one of the tables, pulled out her phone, and called Lisa Packard.

"No, I don't think we've heard from Benjie. Well, his dad hasn't said anything to me. I had a Board of Realtors meeting last night that ran late, and Tim was already gone for work when I got up this morning."

"But Benjamin definitely hasn't come back home?"

"Um, no. He's not here."

Sam got the feeling her question had prompted the woman to walk into her son's bedroom and look around. She couldn't believe a mother didn't show at least a modicum of concern over the situation. She felt impatience rise and wished she were standing in the same room with this nitwit right now.

"Listen! Your son is missing. Do you not get that?"

"Missing? Really, he went on vacation with two friends. That's hardly *missing*. They're together. I'm sure of it."

"How can you be so sure?" Had the woman not been paying *any* attention at all?

"Well …" Her voice took on new strength. "And how is this any of your business? I don't even know who you are, and here you go accusing me of being a bad mother."

If the shoe fits. But Sam held her tongue. She could see this devolving into a verbal catfight with this person she'd never met.

Kelly was watching with wide eyes as Sam ended the call. "Boy, she's a cold one. I've known some gung-ho career women, but none that still didn't care what their kids were up to."

Sam shook her head slowly. "Maybe she figures he's over twenty-one and doesn't need parental monitoring."

"And that's valid too. But I still wonder if we'd get a different attitude if we spoke to Benjamin's father."

"I think I've got the name of his company here in my notes," Sam said. "But is that the best approach? Surely they talk sometimes, and they'll put it together that I ran to him right after arguing with her. Maybe we'll save that one for later."

"True. What about Jacob's mom? She definitely wasn't the type to let go just because her son is now an adult."

Bea Winters answered on the first ring. "Oh. I was hoping it was Jacob."

"So, you haven't heard anything from him yet?" Sam asked, after reintroducing herself and Kelly.

"Not a thing. Ever since your call, I've been thinking about this, hoping the little fight didn't flare up again."

"Little fight? You hadn't mentioned that."

"Oh, I'm sure it's nothing now. Jacob kind of got into it with Casey over something, right before the trip. You know how boys are, especially the ones that have known each other all their lives."

"Well, I only have a daughter, so I'm not sure about boys and their disagreements. What was it about?"

"A girl. Casey's got this girlfriend and he talked about taking her along on the trip. Jacob was opposed. It was a guys' trip, he said. He didn't want this … Amanda's her name. He didn't want her messing up their plans. Plus, he said it would be too crowded in the car for four, plus all their gear. If she went, he would cancel or figure out a way to get there on his own."

A little alarm signal went off in Sam's head. If the three boys actually had split up and traveled separately, it would change a lot of things.

"Is it possible he actually did that? Changed his plans?"

"Oh, I don't think so. I was at the market when they actually left, but all the things Jacob had set out for the trip were gone. His car is in the garage. He would've told me if he was taking the bus or had made another plan."

"Could he and the younger boy, Benjamin Packard, have taken Benjamin's car, gone on their own?"

"Well, now I suppose that's possible … But I don't think so. I just know they're all together."

Sam ended the call after extracting another promise from Bea to let them know if she heard from her son. She looked up at Kelly. "What do you think?"

"Typically, I think young guys resolve their differences with a bunch of harsh words, or maybe a punch or two during a scuffle, then it's all better and they dust themselves off and are best buds again. It's girls who go into a snit over any little thing and hold a grudge forever. Our weapons of choice are the silent treatment and backbiting gossip."

"And about whether the boys changed their travel plans or stuck together?"

"No idea."

"Much as I hate to, I'm calling Lisa Packard back to see if Benjamin has a car and whether it's at home or not. Wanna bet she'll have to go look in the garage to find out?"

Kelly picked up her own phone. "Let me do it."

"Of course, his car is here," Lisa said when Kelly put the question to her. "Where else would it be?"

"Fine, just checking." Kelly hung up. "You're right. She's feeling really defensive about all this." She brushed muffin crumbs from her lap. "So, we're back to the theory that they all came together and it was in Casey's car?"

Sam nodded, but the doubt hung on. There were buses, planes, and trains, although none of these boys sounded like the type to take the initiative and head out alone. Most likely they were together. But what if the fight *hadn't* been put to rest? What if the disagreement had gone beyond bickering and ended up with someone hurt? It could explain a lot toward why none of the boys were in touch with his family in all this time.

Chapter 12

As customers began to fill the bakery, Sam got up, cleared their mugs, and wiped the table. "We should talk to Evan again. You have time for that this morning?"

"Sure. Scott and Ana are planting seeds in cups for her biology lesson. Something about growing tomatoes and cucumbers and having them ready for salads this summer. I have a feeling my kitchen is a mess of potting soil and gardening tools."

"Let's just drive over to his office." Sam donned a light jacket, picked up her bag, and the two of them got into her pickup truck.

It was one of those spring days that the rest of the country takes for granted—bright sunshine, a hint of warmth in the air, the tulips and other bulbs blooming prolifically. Here in town, the flowering trees were showing the first signs of buds. But she knew if they climbed a thousand feet in elevation, up the ski valley road, for instance, there would still be snowy patches and mud aplenty. It was simply the reality of springtime in the mountain regions.

Evan's squad car sat in the back lot on Civic Center Drive, so Sam cruised on past and parked in the public lot. They walked inside and were shown to the back right away.

"It still pays to have connections here," Sam commented.

She greeted Rico and Waters, two deputies who'd been here in Beau's day as sheriff. They asked about their former boss and both had hugs for Sam and Kelly. Evan was sitting behind the desk in his private office and rose when Sam tapped at the door.

"I'm guessing you're here about those three missing young men," he said. "And I'm happy to report there's news."

"Good news, I hope," Kelly said.

He waggled his hand back and forth. "Not sure yet. But I'm pretty sure their car was found yesterday. Red Mustang with California plates. Not lots of those around here. I asked the State Police to hold off having it towed until I can run up there and take a look. I want to see where and how it's parked. See if there's any sign of the kids nearby."

"Where is it?" Sam asked.

"Oh—Questa."

"Really? That's pretty far from TSV and not at all on the route they should have taken."

"Right. Could explain just how lost they really were when they got here."

"Could we ride along?" Kelly asked, her eyes bright

with anticipation.

"Sure. Come on." He led the way out the back door from the squad room to the employee parking lot.

As Evan drove, Sam imagined the route. They passed the turnoff to the Taos Ski Valley and kept heading north. The visitors would have been nearly thirty miles, by road, from their intended destination if they came this way and drove all the way to the little crossroad town of Questa. As hard as it was for a local resident to imagine, she had to keep in mind that these were visitors from out of state, and maybe they didn't have a clue.

Summer Gaines had told Kelly that Casey's Mustang was an older model—not quite vintage muscle car, but more of a classic than the newest ones. It didn't have built-in satellite navigation, she'd confirmed. But the young men hadn't been spotted at the rental cabin, and how did their car end up so far away?

Evan seemed to be following Sam's mental process. "This makes no sense to me. Even someone without a GPS can still read a map, can't they? Okay, scratch that— some can't. But between the three of them, wouldn't these guys have spotted the signs that would tell them where to turn?"

"Young guys, partying on the way, maybe a few beers, a little weed, something …" Kelly suggested, from the back seat.

"True. I've seen it all," he admitted. "You can't assume anything about a person's condition when they're driving."

"When they head out on vacation, they leave their brains at home. Someone who worked at one of the ski areas once told me that," Sam added.

Evan chuckled. "Doesn't surprise me." A garbled burst

of static came over his radio and he turned the volume down. "Anyway, we'll check this out. Gotta decide if it should be impounded. It's not on any stolen vehicle lists. For all we know, this trio got themselves so lost they think they actually ended up where they were supposed to be. Zoned out or stoned, they could be lounging around on someone's deck, perfectly happy to have ditched the idea of snowboarding for a few days."

"Mom, tell him about the phone calls we made this morning."

Sam sat a little straighter. "One of the parents mentioned something, almost in passing, about the boys having some kind of argument right before the trip."

Evan's head snapped toward her. "News to me."

"Right. Us too, until this morning. Supposedly it was over a girl. Not a triangle kind of thing. Seems one guy wanted to bring a girlfriend and the others objected."

"They settle it?"

"Jacob Winters' mother seemed to think so. Her son and Casey Hardwick have known each other since elementary school, and they always ironed out their differences."

They were north of Arroyo Hondo now, driving through an area with sweeping views and nice stands of pine forest. Evan kept his eyes on the curves in the road. "So you think Casey may have split off from the others? Maybe he and the girlfriend drove up here and the other boys aimed for the cabin at TSV but got lost along the way. Do we know who paid for the trip?"

"The same mom who told us about the friction had already said she didn't let them use her card. Casey's sister didn't do it. So that leaves Benjamin Packard's parents. That would be my guess. Unless one of the guys has his own card, one with a high enough limit to cover the whole trip. I can't access anyone's credit records."

Kelly piped up again. "Unless Casey pulled a real sneaky, I don't think the girlfriend was along on the trip. Summer would have said something about it. She talked about Jacob and Casey loading the car, strapping their snowboards on top, and the plan was for them to pick up Benjamin and hit the road."

"Hopefully, once we see the car, we'll be able to tell. Girls leave their own kind of evidence behind."

"What does that mean?" Sam turned in her seat to stare at Evan.

"Well, you know … I mean, every time Riki's in my car I find her sunglasses or a plastic bracelet or something left behind. Plus, the car just smells like her—better than after I've used it."

"Nice catch, but not every woman leaves a trail of things behind."

He was saved from further response as they approached the town. He slowed to a touch below the speed limit and scanned both sides of the road. Compared to Taos, this little town didn't offer a whole lot. It was best known as a jumping-off place to several good hiking trails and to the Rio Grande Gorge, and for the now-defunct open pit molybdenum mine to the east. There was no real town center, just a lot of modest homes clustered around the intersection of two highways. The high school and library sat near the north end; the few restaurants tended to feature burgers or Mexican food. Most travelers buzzed on through, on their way to Colorado.

"The car is in the lot at the El Pinto Motel," Evan said. "Manager called me when it had sat there several days and he couldn't match it up with any of their guests. I asked for the plate number, and it's a match for Casey Hardwick's Mustang."

The El Pinto wasn't much. A strip of ten identically sized rooms and a slightly bigger one with larger windows and a sign above the door that said Office. The whole thing was stuccoed light tan, with a reddish asphalt shingle roof, and doors that sported peeling turquoise paint. They spotted the red Mustang parked beyond the very end of the building, with a layer of dust on it. Evan pulled up beside it.

He climbed out of the cruiser and set his Stetson on his head. "I'm not liking the looks of this. Until we know for sure, treat the vehicle as evidence." He reached down for a box of latex gloves and handed them out to the ladies before pulling on a pair for himself. "Try not to touch, but if you do, make sure you have these on."

He walked to the driver's side door and tugged the handle. It opened. "Good way to get a car stolen," he muttered.

Sam stood on the opposite side, by the passenger door, and peered through the dusty window. No key in the ignition.

"Go ahead and open it," Evan said. "We might as well see what we find inside and get some pictures." He went back to the cruiser for a camera.

"There's a rack on top, but no snowboards," Kelly noticed. "I wonder if the guys took them off or they've been swiped."

Evan snapped a few shots of the car at different angles, including the empty carrier on top and the license plates. From each of the open doors, he got pictures of the interior, which included an Igloo cooler that filled one half of the back seat. No way for four people to fit, along with that, so odds were good the girlfriend had not come along.

"Hold that cooler lid open, Kelly."

She pushed the front seat forward and ducked inside, wrinkling her nose at the scents of males-in-tight-quarters and fast food consumed inside the car. With one finger, she pushed the cooler lid upward. Evan held the camera over it and hit the shutter button. The Igloo held four cardboard carriers for six-packs of beer, three of them empty. Other than empty Doritos bags, soda cups from McDonald's, and crumpled fast food bags from a variety of places, there were no bottles on the floor or anywhere else in the car.

"Great. Afraid of being caught with open containers, they simply tossed the bottles out along the way and littered the highway instead." He muttered something under his breath that sounded like 'dumb law, if you ask me.'

"Key's under the front floormat," Kelly called out. The sheriff snapped two photos of it in place.

Road grime spattered the sides and back of the car and caked the wheel wells and tires, Sam noted. "Looks like they drove through snowy country at some point. There are cinders stuck in the tire tread."

Evan snapped more pictures, including close-ups showing the reddish dirt/gravel mix New Mexico used in place of road salt on slippery roads. Sam was glad to see him taking the discovery seriously. Before today, she'd had the impression that he was hoping the boys had gone elsewhere and this wouldn't become his problem.

A man with stringy hair to his shoulders and tattoos running up the sides of his neck came walking toward them, and Sam gave Evan an elbow to alert him.

"Hi folks, I'm Dan Smith, the manager here. I called you about the car," he said with a nod toward the Mustang.

"Did you see who was driving it when it arrived?" Evan asked after introducing Sam and Kelly.

Smith shook his head. "I was off for a couple days and it was here when I came in on Monday. The other manager said she thought it belonged to the people in Room 1. I don't know ... the way she said it I got the feeling she didn't actually see them drive up in it either. But, you know, that's not all that odd. They park their car, walk in to register, maybe move the car, maybe not. Our registration form asks for a plate number but a lot of people don't remember theirs. I never press 'em."

"How long has it been here?"

A shrug. "Like I said ... I didn't pay it any attention until the folks in number 1 left and the car was still here. Gave it a couple more days, in case it's broke down, out of gas or something. Figured the owner would come and take it away."

Smith stared at the Mustang, as though it was a vehicle he wouldn't mind owning, himself. Then he seemed to realize Evan was watching him. "Course my next thought was it could be stolen—being out-of-state plates and all— so that's when I figured you'd better know about it."

"Thanks. Appreciate that." Evan took down Smith's contact details, along with those of the woman manager who'd been on duty when the car first showed up, saying he'd be in touch if he thought of other questions.

Sam tuned out, scanning the car and the area for any other clues, but the dirt parking area had been disturbed by crisscrossing tracks and gave no indication which direction the Mustang had come from. Weeds at the edge of the lot held a collection of paper scraps, food wrappers, cigarette butts, and smashed aluminum cans, but everything looked as if it had been there for years. Not likely to hold any evidence that could directly tie to the missing young men.

She wandered back to Evan, where he was telling Dan Smith that he would have the car towed to the county impound lot. "If anyone comes around looking for it, give them this number," he said, handing over his business card. "And, you know what—give me a call yourself, if anyone asks about the car. I'd like to know if anybody shows an interest."

"Sure, man." Smith pocketed the card and went back toward the office.

Evan radioed for a county tow truck. Sam's phone vibrated in her pocket and she reached for it.

"Hey, Rupert, how are you?"

"Meh. It's not a great day."

"What's up?"

"Mark. He came by for the last of his stuff, and I—well, it reopened the wound. I've been sitting here for two hours feeling sorry for myself."

"Look, I'm stuck out in Questa for a while. Long story, which I can tell you later, but how about if I come by later? Tea and sympathy sort of thing? Or we meet somewhere for a drink, a drown your sorrows approach?"

There was a silence of several seconds. "Drink would not be a good thing for me right now. Aim for tea, and bring something delectable from your shop. Just text me ahead when you're on the way so I have a minute to clean up my face."

Oh boy. This wasn't good. But at least she knew Rupert's taste in pastry. She called Jen and asked her to set aside a half-dozen almond croissants and a half-dozen assorted brownies—double chocolate, mocha, and turtle. That should do it. She felt a pang of guilt that neither she nor Rupert needed the calories, then justified it by telling herself this was an intervention—serious stuff. She would eat no more than one of each and then use the excuse of mutual dieting to get her friend back on track and lift his mood again.

Chapter 13

Muddy water ran down the driveway, settling in the tire tracks, creating twin streams of muck. Casey paced the cabin like a caged animal, repeatedly staring at his phone screen in hopes that the nonexistent signal would appear. Benjamin watched him warily, waiting for the next explosion. How could the landline *still* be down? he wondered. And how could people live like this—no phone, no internet, and an entire season where it wasn't feasible to get out of one's own driveway?

He'd put the question to Nancy, finding a few minutes when Casey wasn't around.

"Oh, sweetie, it's just our perfect lifestyle. We keep the pantry well stocked, still got half the elk in the freezer from last fall, and you know how it is to keep a house clean. I'm *always* busy."

To prove the point, she sprinkled cleanser in the kitchen sink and began to scrub vigorously. He noticed she'd avoided the question about the landline. Officially, the couple seemed to believe the phone company hadn't gotten a crew out to work on whatever wire had been taken down in the storm, four days ago. He sat at the kitchen counter, his head resting in his hand.

"Go find a book to read. I've got tons of great fiction on those shelves in the rec room," Nancy said, looking up from the perfectly clean sink. "You like Tom Clancy? Got most of his Jack Ryan series."

He'd read them all, but Benjamin supposed he could find something. He trudged down the wooden steps to the basement, where he found Jacob sprawled on the sagging plaid sofa with a video controller in hand and a bag of Cheetos beside him. He crossed in front of the boxy old TV set, eliciting a 'hey!' from Jacob, and scanned the contents of the bookshelves. There was a Grisham legal thriller he hadn't yet read and he pulled it out. He flopped into the big recliner in the corner to read.

Heavy steps thundered on the steps.

Shit. Casey. The perpetual bad mood of the day was back.

* * *

Nancy rinsed the cleanser out of the sink and put the sponge away. How much more cleaning and baking could she do? They were running low on certain food items—cereal, milk, bread, and chips—but Lyle was adamant that they not admit that their four-wheel-drive truck could easily make it to town for some shopping. And how much longer could she go on, staying hyper-vigilant as to the whereabouts of three young men in the house? He'd said not to let them out of her sight, but really. It was getting ridiculous.

She replayed last night's conversation where she again asked him what happened to the boys' car and he stuck with his rant about this Braxton Lab, whatever that was. She needed to get him alone so they could figure out a plan while the boys were occupied downstairs.

Lyle was walking across the yard between the barn and the house. Her perfect chance. She grabbed a sweater and headed for the front door.

Intercepting Lyle before he reached the porch, she hooked an arm around his and steered him back to the barn.

"We need to talk," she said. It wasn't often that she directed the conversation. He was normally the one to say how things would go, but now she needed answers. "I've asked you twice about that car," she began. "Where is it? How are we ever going to get rid of our guests if they can't drive away?"

He positioned himself so he could see out the side window while leaning a hip against his truck. "We can't let 'em get away."

"What? We're going to just keep three young men in our home forever. They've got families who must be worried sick."

"And at least one of 'em is a spy for Braxton Lab."

"I don't even know what that is or why it matters, Lyle."

"Braxton Lab is *supposedly* a manufacturer of vaccines, but I read this report that says they're working on more secretive things. Truth serum, tracking implants. Ways for the gov'ment to learn things about people, to take away our freedoms."

She gave him a sideways look. "And *we* are so important they'd send spies here? Spies disguised as college kids, complete with snowboards and plans for spring break?"

"Spy's no good unless his cover story is believable." He crossed his arms in a huff.

"Lyle, really."

"Okay, the car. I towed it away, the night you first asked me about it. I hitched the tow bar to the truck and pulled the thing over to Questa."

Her eyes widened.

"Left it at some dump motel, figured somebody'd steal it in no time. You know them types up there in the hills. That way, Braxton's tracking device shows the vehicle far, far from here."

She clamped her lips shut.

He seemed to figure out that he'd crossed a line. "I know, honey. It's a tricky situation and I'm still thinking it out. We're okay."

"We started out joking with each other when they pulled up, about how nobody gets their directions right. It seemed harmless enough to bring them in out of the snow and feed them dinner. I thought we'd fool them for a little while and send them on their way in the morning. How did it go this far, Lyle?"

"Stick by me, Nance. That's what we do, hon. We stick together, no matter what."

They did. She'd watched him steadily heading toward this survivalist mentality but she'd stuck by him all the way. Didn't see it changing now that they were both well into their seventies.

He saw her face soften. "We got us plenty of food. We got the—" voice dropping to a whisper, "—gold and cash. We got us lots of protection. We'll be fine."

"Until this whole situation gets so weird the boys figure out a way to report what's happened here."

He stood straighter, squared his shoulders. "What's happened? I mean really, what has happened. We took 'em in, fed 'em, kept 'em warm and safe …"

Isolated them from their friends and families … She didn't say it. Hoped it really would all work out okay in the long run.

"We're running low on groceries."

"Can't let them boys know it's easy enough to drive out of here in the truck. Gotta keep 'em thinking the roads are impassable."

Nancy glanced toward the house, knowing she should get back inside. "Okay, then we'll break into your stash of MREs."

"No! That'll raise suspicion if we're serving military meals." He paced rapidly back and forth, still keeping an eye toward the window. "I'll figure out something. Make a shopping list and I'll figure out what to do."

* * *

"We gotta figure out how to get out of here," Casey said through clenched teeth. "I'm going nuts. Damn. Should have stayed home with Amanda instead of bringing you guys on this lame trip."

"You *brought* us? The whole trip was your idea," Jacob reminded. "We paid our way. Well, we will when the credit card bill comes."

Benjamin kept a wary eye toward the doorway at the top of the stairs. "Where are they right now?"

"She's cleaning the kitchen, enough to qualify it for a hospital. The old man's doing something out in the barn. I was gonna offer to help, just to get outside a little, but he gave me that look."

"The *scaaarryy* look …" Jacob teased in a ghostly voice.

"Shove it." Casey picked up a pillow and threw it.

"Seriously, guys. You also getting the feeling we're being watched 24-7?" Jacob had set down the video controller and was digging into the snack bag.

"Exactly." Casey's mood shifted subtly. "Why else are we still here? And did anyone buy the story about my car getting towed away but no one, no cops, came up here to tell me I had a fine to pay or anything?"

Benjamin stuck his finger between the pages of the book and sat up a little straighter. "Well, the roads *are* bad. You've seen that mud out in the driveway. Can't imagine how it is farther down, where the water's collecting and it's getting all churned up."

"Yeah, right. And the phone? The damn phone hasn't worked in days. I'm betting the old guy cut the wire or something."

Benjamin privately thought Casey was being way overdramatic, but then he heard the front door close with a soft click. He put his finger to his lips.

Chapter 14

Sam put her phone away and walked back toward Evan's cruiser, where he sat fiddling with a little notebook.

"Tow truck's at least forty minutes out," he said. "Sorry to have you stuck here with me. I know, odds of the car just taking off before we get it put away are slim, but I've already not taken this case seriously enough. Can't have this on my head as well. It's time to get the media involved."

Sam was glad to hear him suggest it. Their paltry leads weren't working out, but maybe someone in the area had spotted the young men and could help.

"When I get back to the station, I'll call Mike Garcia at the *Taos News*. He's good, and he can help us get the story out on the news wires, and enlist the help of radio and TV stations, as well." Evan gave a wry grin. "As long as I grant him the exclusive to be the first to report it."

"Seems like a small price for the service," she said, reaching out to pat his arm.

* * *

It was close to noon before they got back to Taos. Kelly was due at Puppy Chic for the afternoon so Sam dropped her off, grabbed the box of goodies Jen had set aside, and decided to take along two generous slices of spinach-mushroom quiche. It would be a good idea to get something nourishing into Rupert before they both went into sugar overload.

"Sorry I couldn't get here any sooner," she said, as she walked into his sweeping living room with the unparalleled view of Taos Mountain.

She set the pastry box on the coffee table and carried the quiche to the kitchen. He trailed along like a lonely puppy in gray pajama pants and a shapeless black pullover. She noticed gaps on the sideboard and on the breakfast area walls where photos of Rupert and Mark as a couple had been.

"Why don't you shower and get dressed while I warm this up," she suggested, locating a baking sheet for the quiche. "And where's the Earl Grey? I'll brew a pot of that too."

While he was out of the room, she heated the oven and slid the baking sheet inside. There wasn't much in the fridge but she found enough usable lettuce and cherry tomatoes to make a little salad for each of them. By the time her friend returned, fifteen minutes later, the table was nicely set (it was fun to bring out pieces of his Lenox and Waterford), and she had subtly shifted his photo collection around to fill the gaps so Mark's absence wasn't so blatantly obvious.

Rupert cleaned up well. His thick gray mane was full and shiny again (although she noted he was due for a trim) and, even though his loose pants and tunic were black, he'd added one of his favorite purple scarves. Progress.

"Smells good in here, Sam." He glanced at the table but didn't comment on the rearrangement of the pictures. "Thanks for doing this."

"We've been friends more than twenty years, Rupe. You know I'm here for you, whether you want to talk about it or just sit and have something to eat."

"You know my sad story. There's nothing more to say, so I vote that we stuff our faces." He slipped an arm around her shoulders and gave a firm hug.

She dished up the quiche and they sat down to the lovely table. Despite his claim of having nothing more to say, Rupert talked about the Caribbean vacation over the holidays and how well everything had gone.

"I just don't know when it turned," he lamented. "I didn't see it coming."

Sam had no clue what to say. All of her own romantic breakups had been her idea. Even Jake Calendar who'd left her pregnant in Alaska. She wouldn't have stayed with him whether he begged her to or not. Sitting here with Rupert, it was best to say nothing. If she blasted Mark for his insensitivity, how would it go if they ever got back together again? Not in Sam's favor, she would bet. So she simply let him talk.

Once the quiche was gone, they carried their tea to the living room and broke into the pastries. An almond croissant followed by a large brownie calmed Rupert, and he sank back against the puffy sofa cushions.

"Enough about me and my woes. Someday there will be a book in this, but I'm not ready yet," he said, taking a sip of his Earl Grey. "You mentioned working on a new case? Some missing persons?"

Sam nodded and set half of her brownie back on her plate. "This morning, Evan got a call about the young man's car being found. Kelly and I drove up to Questa with him to check it out. I'm not sure that's a promising lead, but it's the first trace we've had in knowing the boys were at least in the region. Evan's having to admit now that they didn't merely change plans and dash off to Las Vegas. Still, if they ended up at a Questa motel instead of a cabin in Taos Ski Valley, that's pretty far off track."

He nodded and reached for the teapot to refill their cups.

Sam heard her phone and reached for her messenger bag to retrieve it. An unfamiliar local number was on the screen. Scam or important? She took the call.

"Brenda Appleton, at Taos Ski Valley operations," said the voice. "You were here the other day, asking about three visitors and whether they bought tickets?"

"Oh, right." Sam had nearly spaced out that conversation, with everything else that had happened since. "Did you find anything?"

"Afraid not. None of those three names showed up on our signed waivers."

"And the boys couldn't have purchased lift tickets without signing that first? Is there any way that step could have been missed?"

Brenda lowered her voice. "Well, not officially. I won't swear that it never happens when someone has a buddy who works the lifts … but with out-of-state visitors, that would be nearly unheard of."

Sam thanked her and hung up.

"So, the boys never checked in at their rental cabin, never got tickets for the lifts, and their car ended up more than twenty miles from where they were supposed to be," she mused aloud to Rupert.

"You've definitely got a mystery on your hands. Say, did you ever get a chance to talk with that friend of mine who has the big house up there?"

When she shook her head, he promptly picked up his phone, tapped out the number, and over the speaker he asked Sam to relate the story to the woman who answered.

Unsurprisingly, she knew nothing about the three young men. "I see so many people milling about, after a while it's a blur. Spring break is especially crazy up here, and I often just tune it out. A red Mustang might have caught my eye, but I definitely don't remember one of those in the past few weeks."

"Okay, thanks." Sam couldn't imagine the boys making it as far as the ski area, and then turning around and taking the car all the way to Questa anyway. But it had been worth a shot to ask the question.

She wished Rupert luck with the book deadline and he wished her luck with the case before she picked up her bag and headed home for the day.

Beau was on the front porch, scraping mud off his boots with a stick. He let go with a mild curse when the stick broke just as Sam got out of her truck. She stared at him to see what was the matter—as with most ranchers, bad language was a rarity. It was one of the reasons she couldn't watch Western movies of the current era. Real cowboys rarely uttered a word worse than 'damn' and those Hollywood types just did not get that.

"The mud will brush off easier after it's dry," she suggested.

"So true." He slid the boots off and walked into the house in his socks.

The dogs followed, leading their humans straight to the pantry, where the bag of kibble waited.

"I ate way too much at Rupert's this afternoon," she told Beau. "Would we be okay with tomato soup for dinner?"

"Add a grilled cheese sandwich to my plate, and I'd love it. I'll even cook it." He gave her a kiss as she shrugged out of her jacket.

They heated the soup and settled with trays in front of the fireplace and TV. Beau flipped to one of the Albuquerque news stations first. The lead story was about the missing young men who had headed for Taos and not been seen since. The familiar photos of Casey Hardwick, Jacob Winters, and Benjamin Packard stayed on the screen as the announcer talked.

"Wow, that was quick," Sam said, taking a spoonful of her soup. "Evan just got the word out this morning."

Beau teased her about how it wouldn't be called news if it didn't get out right away, and she tossed a bread roll at him. But inside, she was relieved that now the news was out, maybe someone in the community would give them a solid lead.

As soon as the weather report was over, Beau switched over to a documentary on another channel. The show focused on survivalists who set up remote camps in places like Montana, where the journalist had embedded himself to gain material on the lifestyle. The reporter made the point that while many initially joined these groups in order to learn the skills it would take to survive a natural disaster, others were convinced the government would soon fall apart and only those who were adequately prepared would survive the ensuing chaos.

Paranoia and anti-government sentiment seemed prevalent among those he talked with, as they showed him stockpiles of preserved food, enough to last twenty-five years if it came to that, along with water, medical supplies, and—inevitably—weapons. The leaders of the group made some convincing arguments in favor of preparedness. It was those men and women on the fringe who seemed worrisome.

As the final credits rolled, Sam stood and gathered their bowls and spoons. "Wow, sounds pretty dangerous."

"Don't let the doomsday tone worry you," Beau said as he folded the trays and carried them to the hall closet. "Not every one of these turns into a Ruby Ridge or anything close."

"That seemed to be what the reporter was focusing on."

"As they most often do. A story isn't a story without some element that'll make people scared or angry."

"And you know this, how?"

"Let's just say you'd be surprised that the survivalist movement isn't limited to bearded, backwoods men in Montana. They're everywhere. Lots of ordinary people want to be prepared, for anything from a natural disaster to a full-blown rebellion against the government."

"Well, the people in that camp they just showed definitely seemed to be leaning toward the latter." She stacked the bowls in the kitchen sink and ran hot water into them.

"Would the reporter have found his story if he'd chosen an ordinary suburban neighborhood in Denver? No. Well, maybe. But it would have been a whole different tone without the beards and off-grid lifestyle." He opened the dishwasher and, while Sam was dropping the utensils in, he covered the butter dish and put away the remaining rolls.

She could see his point. For the same reason moviemakers felt the need to include dirty-mouthed cowboys, documentary makers needed to focus on something frightening. She relaxed her shoulders and gave her common-sense husband a smile.

He kissed her forehead and turned toward the doorway to the living room. "Is that your phone I hear?"

It was Kelly's ringtone, and Sam dashed for it.

Chapter 15

"Sorry—I know it's late and you guys are probably settled in," Kelly started.

"No problem. What's up?"

"It has to do with the Mustang, and if you don't want to talk about the case during your evening ..."

"It's *fine*. Spill it."

"So, I noticed a parking sticker on the windshield and I snapped a picture of it. It was issued by a company called Braxton Lab. When I got home I looked them up. They produce vaccines, primarily, and I wondered if maybe Casey Hardwick worked there. You know, an internship or something."

"Good thinking. Maybe if he didn't report to his family, he might have called in at work?"

"I had that thought, even though who would do that?

But I called them and asked for HR."

"And?"

"No record of Casey Hardwick as an employee or even as an intern or part-timer. The sticker has a number on it, so I enlarged the photo until I could read it and gave the HR person that info. Turns out the employee who was issued that sticker left the company several years ago. I should have guessed—the car is a 2010 model, so not exactly new."

"If a company issues specific parking assignments, it seems they would ask for that sticker back when the employee leaves."

"Right. They normally do, according to HR, but the lady admitted to me that it doesn't always happen. Although the sticker also serves as admittance through the facility's entry gate, not just anyone can get in by that means alone. I asked how that would work. For instance, if the sticker stays with the car and the driver tries to come back into the facility, they'd still have to have their current employee photo ID."

"And if the car sold—say to somebody like Casey Hardwick—he doesn't automatically have access to Braxton's facility or parking lot."

"Exactly. I guess that's why they don't stress too much over it. She said they would have asked for their former employee's assurance that the sticker had been removed from the car and destroyed."

"But no guarantee that it actually happened."

"And that's why the sticker is still on the car."

"That's some great detective work, Kel. Proud of you."

"What do you say I take it even one step further? I'll call Evan and see if he'll use his law enforcement influence with the California motor vehicles department to trace the ownership of the car."

"I don't know if that will prove anything pertinent to our investigation, but it couldn't hurt."

"Just thinking, it might be good to know how long Casey has owned the car. I already asked Summer and she didn't seem to know when he got it, just 'sometime in the past two or three years' she said. If he's had it a long time, probably all the DNA or trace evidence belongs to him and his friends. But if something ... well, something unthinkable ... has happened to the boys, Evan will need to order a full forensic investigation on the car, and other DNA could show up in there."

"Wow. Thorough of you."

"Probably he'll just think I watch too much *CSI*." Kelly gave a little chuckle. "Which I do. Okay, I'm going to call him now before it gets too late."

Sam smiled as she clicked off the call. Her little detective.

* * *

Sam walked into the sales room, carrying a tray of sliced quick-breads—lemon, carrot, honey-bran, and mocha chip—for the breakfast crowd. As she slid the tray into the display case, she caught sight of the large jar where customers were putting their entry slips for the gingerbread-scene prizes.

"Lots of entries already," she commented to Jen.

"People are really getting into this. I had to make it a rule that it's one entry per customer, per visit. We had a few who were so enthused they wanted to 'stuff the ballot box,' so to speak."

Sam hadn't thought of that.

"Anyway, it's getting them back in. A few are bringing their kids, to get more entries, but I figure that's okay. The kids always talk their moms into buying something extra. A cup of coffee turns into coffee and a dozen cookies. Sales are picking up, and we're seeing new faces."

Sam walked to the front window to check the display, make sure nothing had slipped out of place, and she spotted Evan Richards' cruiser in front of Puppy Chic. The sheriff was just stepping out of his vehicle with a paper sack in his hand. She stepped outside and got his attention.

"Oh, hey, Sam." He held up the bag. "Riki forgot her lunch when she left the house this morning."

"I just wanted to thank you for including Kelly and me when you located Casey Hardwick's car yesterday."

"No problem. I guess Kelly told you she called me last night with another idea about that?"

"Yeah, I hope it leads somewhere. Somewhere valid, I mean."

"You never know. We follow a lot of leads that go nowhere, and then—boom—something proves to be just the thing that breaks a case wide open."

She raised an eyebrow, questioning.

He glanced toward Puppy Chic. "I haven't even been to my office yet, Sam. But I'll get on this. I should be able to get into a database of motor vehicle owners. I pulled the VIN from the Mustang and I'll find out how long Hardwick has owned the car and if there's any tie between him and the previous owner."

"Thanks, Evan. Beau and I saw the story about the boys on Channel 4 last night."

"Yeah, we did too. Looks like Mike Garcia's story made it to the main statewide media outlets. Could even go regional or national, if this drags on much longer." He caught her eager expression. "Just don't get too hopeful. Like I said, a lot of leads end up going nowhere."

She smiled and patted his arm. "Take Riki her lunch and get back to your day. Sorry if this turns out to be a rabbit trail."

She walked back through the crowded sales room, making certain Jen was handling the counter fine on her own, before joining Becky again in the kitchen. Three large racks of cut-out cookies had come out of the oven and were cooling. Bunnies, chicks, and eggs needed glazes and piped decoration. With only a few days to go before Easter, the seasonal designs were in demand.

"I'll take bunnies and chicks if you'll do the eggs," Becky said with a grin.

"Because the eggs need the most piping?"

"Well …"

"No problem. If you finish first, you can decorate that flowerpot birthday cake. The customer wants tulips in at least four different colors."

"I'm on it. I made the tulips out of white modeling chocolate yesterday—tinted yellow, purple, pink, and red—so icing and assembly is no problem."

An hour later, Sam was putting the finishing touches on the Easter egg cookies—a dusting of edible silver sugar over the pastel surfaces of certain ones—when her phone rang. Kelly.

"Evan got back to me about the car." Her voice sounded excited and a little full of pride. Here she was, helping the sheriff with a case! "I got the name of the person Casey bought the car from. It's the son of the man who worked at Braxton Lab."

"So, there was a connection … interesting."

"Evan didn't seem all that excited about it. He got a call while he was talking to me—a jewelry store on the plaza just got robbed! Can you believe it? Anyway, he said I could go ahead and call the seller of the car and see if there's any reason for him to follow up later."

"A robbery, here in Taos. Wow."

"Mom, focus. I get to ask some real questions, and it's okay to say I'm calling on behalf of the sheriff. That's kind of cool, isn't it?"

"It is, Kel. That's great."

"Evan kind of covered what types of questions to ask, so I'm going to make the calls now."

Sam smiled. So cute. "You'll have to fill me in."

Chapter 16

Sam was carrying the flowerpot birthday cake, all boxed up and ready for the customer, when Kelly walked into the sales room.

"Are you late for work at Riki's?" she asked, setting the cake on the back counter with the order sheet attached to the top of the box.

"Nope. I'm not on the schedule today. I'm here to fill you in and thought I'd see if you were interested in a late lunch at Lambert's."

Sam paused for a second on her way to check the beverage bar. "We're swamped right now, Kel, and as much as I love Lambert's, it's not to be rushed. We'll have to find a day when we can take a table out in the patio and really sit back for an enjoyable time. After Easter?"

"You have to eat something. How about Umberto's

taco truck?"

Sam had to laugh. In terms of atmosphere, the two suggestions were at opposite ends of the spectrum, but she had to admit Umberto made fantastic tacos. And they could pick up a few and eat them at a picnic table while they discussed the case, which had to be Kelly's whole point in making the lunch suggestion.

"If you don't mind riding in the bakery van and making a stop to deliver a wedding cake before we eat …"

Kelly helped to carry the four-tier cream and gold confection, and they got the cake secured in the back of Sam's van. The church hall, where the reception would begin in five hours' time, was unlocked. A matronly lady met them and assured Sam she would be there all afternoon to watch the cake.

"Okay," Sam said to Kelly as she started the van, "let's grab our tacos and you can tell me what you learned. I'm hoping the most difficult decision I need to make in the next fifteen minutes is 'chicken or beef.'"

A chilly spring wind had picked up, so they opted to carry their food to the van and eat where they could enjoy its cozy protection. Wrappers crinkled and the meaty smell of Umberto's special recipe filled their senses as they took their first bites.

"Anyway," Kelly said, picking up in the middle of her earlier thoughts, "I called the former Braxton Lab employee who owned the Mustang. His name is Clayton Green. He was friendly enough until I brought up Casey Hardwick's name, asking if Casey had bought the car."

Sam turned in her seat to face Kelly. "What did he say?"

"Okay, this isn't verbatim, but basically he called Casey a smartass punk."

"He formed that opinion based on selling him a car? Okay."

"Apparently, he had more interaction with Casey than that. Sorry, I should have started at the beginning. Mr. Green's son—Foster is his name—was, or is, a friend of Casey's. When Casey found out Mr. Green was thinking of selling the Mustang, they talked. Of course, the father wanted top dollar for the car, which was already almost ten years old, and he set the price accordingly. And he'd had no offers. So, Foster mentioned the car to Casey, and that's when he began to pester Mr. Green to lower the price."

"And I'm guessing he wasn't exactly respectful …"

"Sounds like he wasn't at all." Kelly crumpled the wrapper from her first taco and opened a second. "He had cash in hand, which tempted the older man, who'd had a hard time finding a job that paid as much as Braxton had. Anyway, I got an earful but long story short, Casey talked him down on the price and then wanted him to throw in extras, such as having the car detailed before he would pay for it."

Sam rolled her eyes. "I bet that went over well."

"It's been more than two years, and the old man is still on a rant."

"Did you get the impression Casey Hardwick has an enemy there?"

Kelly chewed thoughtfully for a moment. "Um, not to the extent that this guy would follow him on a trip and do away with him, no. It was probably just a case of him venting to me because his own family is fed up with hearing about it."

"I wonder if Casey is still friends with Foster Green."

"I'm not sure the father would have an accurate

measure of that, but I did get a phone number for Foster. Left him a voice message."

"So, going back to the negotiations, you said Casey demanded that Green have the car detailed before he'd hand over the cash, so I'm assuming he did that."

"Oh yeah. That was another whole rant—what a professional detail job costs these days. He was not happy, but he needed the money."

"Well, it does answer whether Green would have left any trace evidence in the car." Sam stared out the front windshield and sipped at her soda. "If and when Evan has a forensic team go over it, he'll want to know this, so it's good that you got that information."

"Yes, I would think anything they find would have to be evidence from Casey and his immediate circle of friends—or someone who may have carjacked the Mustang and left the boys … Well, I don't want to think about that."

"Give Evan all the names, numbers, addresses—whatever you learned."

"I think I'll call Summer back, bring up those names, and see if she can add anything to the story."

"Good idea." Sam reached for the ignition key and started the van. "I need to get back to work. After this weekend, I should be able to relax a little and be of more help to you."

"It's okay. I'm enjoying this." Kelly bagged their trash and stepped out to place it in the bin provided next to the taco truck. When she got back in the van, she thought of something else. "I keep getting the impression that Casey is sort of an instigator, the smart-mouth type who sets people off."

Sam looked both ways and pulled onto Paseo Pueblo

del Sur. "Mr. Green wasn't the first person to mention something like that, was he?"

"So, what if there was some kind of road rage incident along the trip? Casey could have got into an altercation with another driver … maybe they were followed …?"

"If another vehicle was harassing them, hot on their tail, it could explain how they totally missed the turn to the ski valley and ended up in Questa instead." And then what happened? Things could have gotten very ugly.

"I'll mention all this to Evan and see what he says. I have a feeling he'll take it as pure speculation."

"Unless the car provides some evidence of it."

"True." Ice rattled in Kelly's soda cup as she sucked down the last of her soda.

"But maybe he'd be willing to check with law enforcement in the surrounding towns and counties, see if the boys ever called for help or reported an incident."

They pulled into the alley behind the bakery and parted ways, Kelly heading home and Sam switching mental gears from crime-solving to making Easter bunny cupcakes. As she washed up and prepared a batch of white buttercream frosting, she found herself dwelling on the situation with the three missing boys. How did three young men vanish without a trace, while their car seemed relatively unscathed, miles from where it should be? And what about the man back in California who still harbored bitter feelings toward Casey Hardwick? Could he have something to do with all this?

Chapter 17

Sam heard familiar voices out in the sales room as she set the finished bunny cupcakes onto a tray. It was the time of afternoon when schoolkids stopped in on their way home, and women who'd been shopping wanted a break for a cup of tea and a scone or some other little sweet treat. She carried the cupcakes out front, delighted to see her best friends Zoë and Darryl Chartrain.

She slid the laden tray into the glass display case and then enveloped Zoë in a hug.

"I almost never see you two out and about at this time of day. Come on, take a minute to sit down with a coffee. Cookies are my treat."

Zoë shook her head ruefully. "We can't stay but a minute. I came in to get coffee cake for our guests who are arriving within the hour." Their bed and breakfast kept them hopping, especially with a holiday weekend approaching.

"And I need to run over to the bookstore," Darryl said. "But don't be long. Ivan's already got my order. All I need to do is pay for it and pick up the book."

"Five minutes," Zoë insisted. She turned to Sam while Jen boxed up a cinnamon bundt ring. "Looks like you're as busy as we are, Sam. What's the big jar full of paper slips for?"

Sam explained about the contest for the gingerbread cottage and the little chapel. "You should enter the drawing."

Zoë waved off the idea. "Oh gosh, I've got so much stuff in the house already. I have no idea what I'd do with one of them. But I'll tell you what—I will send our guests over and tell them about it. They've got two young kids, and I'm sure they will be good for some business for you, especially after they've had your coffee cake in the morning and slices of your amaretto cheesecake for tonight's dessert."

Sam spotted Darryl walking back from the bookshop next door. "We need some catch-up time."

"I know. I hear you're working on some kind of a missing person case right now."

"Wow, word travels."

"Not really. Of course, I'd heard the news on the radio earlier, but didn't realize you were involved until I ran into Kelly at the supermarket thirty minutes ago." Zoë handed her credit card over to Jen.

Darryl pushed the front door open, making the overhead bells tinkle. "Sorry, but—"

"I know. We're running late," Zoë said.

Sam helped carry the two large boxes out to Darryl's pickup truck. "One of these days, we *will* take a breather, both of us."

They took a moment for a quick hug, but Darryl was already starting the truck. Sam stepped back and waved. Zoë blew her a kiss.

Inside, all the bistro tables were filled now, and Sam remembered that she'd meant to check supplies at the beverage bar. The rest of the afternoon zipped by until Sam finished the last of tomorrow morning's birthday cakes and carried it to the walk-in fridge. When she went to the sales room to see if Jen had taken any new orders, she found her turning over the Closed sign in the window. The golden glow of early evening lit the adobe buildings on the plaza, a block away.

"You've worked like a dog all day," Jen told her. "Get home and relax."

"We've all been pushed a bit extra this week. But it feels good."

"Better to be busy than sitting around. Not that we've ever had that problem here in the bakery," Jen said with a smile. "My last job, at that gallery … way too many idle hours. I love it here."

Jen retrieved her light jacket from the back room and headed out. Becky had left earlier, and Sam had barely noticed. Julio was mixing dry ingredients for the morning pastries, which he sealed into large tubs. He brushed flour off his hands and wished Sam a good night.

She double checked the locks and the nighttime lighting and was out in her truck before she realized she'd made no plans at all for dinner. They hadn't done a bake-it-yourself pizza in a long time, so she headed for her favorite market to pick one up.

The parking lot was always crowded but she lucked into a spot that wasn't a huge hike to the front doors. Inside, the cashier lines were long, but she hurried to the pizza area and picked out Beau's favorite—the kind with everything. By the time she joined the lineup for self-checkout, she spotted someone she knew.

Evan Richards was fumbling to get the scanner to read a wrinkled package of some sort.

"Doing okay there, sheriff?" Sam teased, carrying her pizza to the adjoining station.

He brightened slightly, spotting her. Just then the machine *bleeped* to let him know his purchase had been scanned.

"Hey, Kelly stopped by right after lunch," he said. "Gave me some names to check out. I haven't had time to get back to her."

"I can pass along the message."

"I was hoping you'd say that." He bagged his two items and stepped over to the station where Sam had already scanned her pizza and was waiting on credit card approval.

As soon as she had her receipt in hand, they walked toward the exit together.

"I haven't had a chance to speak with the guys at the impound garage, to see if there was damage to the Mustang, something indicative of a road rage incident we might have missed," he said. "But Kelly gave me a couple of names for some California residents. I reached a Los Angeles County deputy who looked them up. No wants or warrants on either Clayton Green or his son."

"Which isn't too surprising," Sam said as they crossed the space between the big market and the parking lot.

"They're probably basically law-abiding citizens. Mr. Green seems to have a temper—there were a few calls where his name came up. One from a neighbor who said he overheard a loud verbal altercation at the Green house. The wife wouldn't talk much and didn't press charges. Another time, the son was brought in to answer whether his father had made threats. The kid wouldn't talk and he was over eighteen, so there was no social services involvement. I asked the deputy to keep an ear open. Let me know if he hears of anything else."

They'd reached Sam's truck and stopped at the rear bumper.

"It sounds as though Green, if not criminally liable, does have a tendency to scream at people. That's what Kelly heard, in regard to the auto sale between him and Casey Hardwick, that it got a little ugly."

"That's my impression too. I'll keep checking, and I need to find out whether he has an alibi for the dates when Casey and his friends were last in contact with their families. It may be nothing, or it could lead us to the truth. We'll see."

Sam wished him a good night and sent her best to Riki, then climbed into her truck and headed north. Lights were on in the house and Beau's ranch truck sat in its normal spot. She hoped he'd received her text about the pizza.

He greeted her with a kiss and said he'd already preheated the oven. When he took the pizza to the kitchen, saying he would get it started, she used the time to place a quick call to Kelly and pass along Evan's information about Clayton Green.

"Wow, sounds like he would absolutely be the kind of guy who might start a road-rage thing with someone, doesn't he?"

"It wouldn't surprise me, but I have to wonder about the coincidence of an encounter with Casey, and how that would tie in with the car ending up so far away from California."

Sam laid her phone on the dresser with the speaker on while she changed from her bakery clothes into soft pajama bottoms and a light pullover.

"Anyway, Evan says he'll alert the personnel at the impound yard and have them look for any evidence which could point in that direction. And he's going to follow through and ask for alibis for the Greens and see if he can verify them."

They agreed there wasn't much more they could do at this point.

"I'll stick with Evan, though," Kelly said, "and see what else comes to light."

From downstairs, the sound of the oven timer alerted Sam that dinner was ready. "Gotta go."

"Mom, one other thing? I had Ana with me the other day and she saw the gingerbread house you created for your window display …"

"And she wants it."

"I know, you can't award the prize to your own granddaughter. That wouldn't be right. But maybe if you got in a really creative mood, you could make one for us for Easter?"

"I'd love to. But no promises. It's turning into a crazy week."

Chapter 18

Lyle cornered Nancy in their bedroom right after dinner. "Okay, I got us a plan," he whispered, even though the bedroom door was closed and the boys were down in the basement watching a movie on the old TV set.

"Does it involve groceries? I tell you, I had no idea how much three boys can eat." She carried a stack of folded laundry to the dresser and pulled a drawer open.

Lyle had walked into the connecting bathroom. "We got some of that PM headache medicine, the one I hate to take but you bought it anyway?" He'd pulled open a lower cabinet door and was pawing through the cleaning supplies she kept there.

"Hold on, hold on. I'll get it. You'll have everything in the place all messed up." She set the laundry basket inside the closet and walked into the bathroom.

Behind the mirrored medicine cabinet door, she located the bottle he was talking about and handed it over to him.

"You having a hard time sleeping, honey?" Concern was written all over her face. Lyle always had a hard time sleeping. It wasn't in his nature to be less than vigilant about what was going on around him.

"Not me. I'm fine. We're gonna share this with our guests," he said with a sly grin.

"They'll all take some pills just because you recommend them?"

"They don't need to know *why* they're getting such a good night's sleep."

"What! No. No, no, *no*. You can*not* drug those boys. I won't have it." She reached for the bottle but he was quicker, stepping backward into the bedroom and holding it behind his back.

"You want your groceries, or don't you?" With his other hand, he pulled the slip of paper from his jeans' pocket. "We'll get them sound asleep and I'll be able to drive out without them hearing a thing. That all-night supermarket won't be crowded at midnight tonight and I can do it in no time."

"Oh, Lyle … why can't this just be over? Just let the kids go."

He stepped in closer and his face contorted with fury. "I *told* you why!" His voice hissed through clenched teeth. "At least one of 'em's a spy from Braxton. I haven't figured out yet how this'll go, but we can't take the chance that they'll bring the Feds in here. It don't take much to start another Ruby Ridge or Waco."

Her resolve crumpled. There was no point in arguing with him when he got this way.

"You're gonna make up some of that hot chocolate they like so much. Crush up three of these pills for each cup."

"The dose is two—"

"I *said* three. They're big boys. Take their cocoa down there and watch 'em drink up." He saw the hesitation on her face. "Fine—I'll help you. Let's get in the kitchen now."

Thirty minutes later, all three boys were dozing in their seats as the DVD movie came to an end. Nancy gently ushered them to their bedroom and wished them goodnight. Lyle locked the door from the outside and gave her a satisfied smile.

* * *

Benjamin rolled over in bed and groaned. Light was showing around the curtain, but why did his head feel so fuzzy? He scooted to the edge of his bunk and looked down at Jacob, who seemed dead to the world. On the bed across the room, Casey lay on his back, mouth open, and an undignified snore rattled the room. It was as if the guy hadn't rolled over even once during the night. Benjamin closed his eyes again and drifted off.

He wasn't sure how much time had passed when he woke again, this time a little clearer in the head. The light at the window was brighter. He'd had the strangest dreams. In one, he was sure he'd heard someone at the bedroom door, and Nancy had stood there watching them for a few minutes. In another, he dreamed the scent of bacon cooking and pancakes on the griddle, and he would pour a big puddle of syrup onto his plate …

He opened his eyes and sniffed deeply. That last dream

might actually be real. The bacon smell was definitely in the air. He slid his legs over the edge of the bunk and dropped lightly to the floor. Slipping into his jeans and sweatshirt, he went into the bathroom and brushed the cottony feel from his mouth, swished the toothpaste around and spat, then drank two full cups of the amazingly cold tap water. His head felt clearer.

He carried his shoes with him, heading toward the kitchen, and the bacon smell was definitely real now.

"Good morning, Benjie," Nancy said with a smile.

She was so nice, he couldn't bring himself to tell her he hated that nickname.

"I dreamed about pancakes. But I was afraid it couldn't be real. I thought you said you were out of eggs."

"Oh, I found an extra dozen in the cold-storage pantry. I'd forgotten they were there. Milk and orange juice too. Want some?"

"Maybe some coffee first. I had the hardest time waking up this morning. And the other guys—"

"Oh, that's the mountain air for you. We all sleep really well up here."

That's what they'd been told for days now, but … He couldn't wrap his head around the rest of that thought, so he accepted the mug she handed him.

"Is Lyle up already?"

"Oh, yes. My husband never does sleep in. I tell you, he's always busy with something." She turned back to the skillet filled with bacon, somehow unwilling to look him in the eye.

Maybe that was just his imagination. He took a tentative sip of his coffee then let a big gulp of it scald its way down his throat. He could actually feel his heart rate pick up and his brain begin to unfog.

Jacob wandered into the kitchen, barefoot despite the chilly wood floors, wearing pajama pants and a t-shirt, yawning and scratching idly at his belly. His tousled hair and heavy-eyed face reminded Benjamin of his own sluggish start to the day.

Nancy read the situation and handed Jacob a full mug—doctored with his standard two sugars—without his having to ask. He plopped down at the kitchen table and sipped slowly, barely opening his eyes or acknowledging anyone.

"Would you boys like your pancakes now, or shall we wait for Casey?" Nancy had removed the bacon from the skillet, placing the dozen strips on folded paper towels, which she transferred to a baking sheet and stuck into the oven to keep warm.

Jacob gave a halfhearted shrug—a sure sign he wasn't feeling normal. Benjamin blessed Nancy with a smile and a nod, and she ladled four neat rounds of batter onto the hot griddle. By the time the first four hotcakes were done, Jacob had finished his coffee, perked up, and requested pancakes of his own.

Benjamin was swabbing syrup with the last wedge of his pancake, debating whether to ask for seconds, when heavy footsteps sounded in the hallway. Casey was up. From his chair at the table, Benjamin saw his friend cross the living room and stare out the front windows. Casey's eyes narrowed and his fists clenched.

"What the hell!" he yelled, spinning. He stomped into the kitchen and stared at Nancy. "What the ever lovin' hell!"

Her eyes went wide and she took a step back from the

stove. "What do you mean, Casey? What on earth is the matter?"

"There's tire tracks! They go right down the driveway. You told us it was too muddy for a vehicle to get in or out of here. So what the f—?"

The front door crashed open. Lyle crossed the open space in three steps and grabbed the neck of Casey's shirt.

"You watch your language, you whippersnapper. You will *not* speak to my wife that way!" His other hand, fisted tightly, swung back ready to deliver a punch.

Completely taken by surprise, Casey backed down. But not by much. He spun on Lyle. "Okay, then, old man. You explain it. How come we can't get out of here, when somebody obviously has?" He drew himself up to his full height, a full five inches taller than Lyle, and the older man took a step back.

Nancy, wiping her hands on her apron, came forward. "Now, you two. Calm down. Let's don't make this into a big problem." She gave her husband a significant look, then turned to Casey. "It's true that we weren't able to get out because of the mud. Then, last night a neighbor gave it a try. He was worried about us up here alone and came to bring a few groceries. Nearly got his truck stuck. Said the bottom of the driveway is pure muck."

Watching with wide eyes, Benjamin thought Lyle looked relieved; Casey only looked skeptical. At least when he responded, his tone was a lot less angry.

"Okay then, if the neighbor can get in, you can get your truck out. I—we—want you to take us to town so we can call someone. I gotta find out where my car went."

Lyle raised a hand to protest but Nancy shut him down with some kind of signal between them.

"Let's all have some food," she suggested, "and then we'll talk about it."

Like a teacher with a class of unruly kids, she pointed her finger and directed them to seats at the table. Casey sat opposite Benjamin. Lyle muttered something about finishing a project and stomped out of the room.

"It'll just take a minute to get you boys more pancakes." Nancy set a mug of black coffee before Casey, as if he needed more energy than he already had, and went to immediately ladling more batter onto the griddle.

The tension in the room went down by a good five notches.

* * *

"You can't just keep the conversation light and give the boys a ride to town?" Nancy whispered.

She'd left the three young men at the kitchen table with enough food to keep them busy a while and had gone in search of her husband. He started at the sound of her voice and looked guiltily up from what he was doing.

"Don't open this door when there's anyone else in the house," he reminded.

"Well, I knew you'd be in here." She kept her voice low as she stepped through the narrow doorway and closed it behind her.

Lyle turned to the stacks of cash he'd carefully counted and piled on the shelves against the back wall of the secret room. To the left were heavy metal shelving units containing cartons of freeze-dried food, drinking water, emergency blankets, charcoal, and gel fuel. On the floor sat a three-foot-square safe, which was loaded with silver and gold bars, bullion coins, and a cache of loose gemstones he'd collected by selling off old jewelry a piece at a time. On his right were three narrow shelves containing boxes of ammunition and five handguns, and leaning against the wall in a custom rack of their own were ten hunting rifles.

Nancy barely gave a glance to the room's contents. It had all been here for years, stored against the day when the government would inevitably invade and try to take away their rights.

"I stopped by Frank's last night, before I went to the supermarket," he said, restacking two bundles of twenty-dollar bills. "He says the sheriff has been asking around about the missing boys."

"Oh, Lyle. I had this feeling we shouldn't—"

His expression stopped her cold.

"You're the one who wanted to bring 'em in, feed 'em. Keep mothering those boys way longer than necessary."

"The weather didn't exactly—"

"I know. Everything just went to shit. I'm figuring this out. I still think that one kid knows more than he's saying, that he's been sent here from Braxton Labs."

She laid a gentle hand on his forearm. "Even if he is, what has he actually got on us? Nothing. We're just this nice couple who took them in out of the storm and gave them a warm place to stay. If you take them to town today, let them be on their way, there's no harm done. He might have a story about being stuck in the cabin here, but who's going to think any worse of us? Nobody."

He grumbled a little but had already calmed down. "I suppose."

"I'll go back to the kitchen and suggest they pack their things and we'll help them get to town. They know they've already missed their dates for the vacation rental, and they'll be eager to get back to California as soon as they report the car stolen and can rent another one to get home with." She looked firmly at him. "Make sense?"

He nodded halfheartedly. She opened the hidden door and stepped out.

* * *

"So … you think you convinced the old guy to give us a ride to town?" Jacob asked Casey as he stuffed the last of his pancakes into his mouth.

A shrug in response. "Prob'ly."

Benjamin carried his empty plate and mug to the sink and lowered them into the soapy dishwater. "I'm going to find Nancy and make sure everything's okay. We'll get a ride and we can start packing our stuff."

He walked down the long hall toward the bedrooms, spotting a coat closet door standing halfway open. He'd just stepped around it when Nancy ducked out. Beyond her, framed in a square of light, was a second opening. There stood Lyle, and when he realized Benjamin had seen him, he reached for a gun.

Chapter 19

"D on't forget the Chocoholics are meeting this afternoon," Becky said when Sam walked into the kitchen.

"Oh yikes. I'd forgotten that they didn't skip this week. Sometimes they do, when a holiday is coming up." The Chocoholics Unanimous book club that met at the shop next door were avid fans of chocolate, mystery novels, and cats—pretty much in that order. For years now, Ivan Petrenko had paid well for Sam to create a delectable dessert for every meeting. Any item, any design—as long as it was all chocolate.

"At least it's easy to think of a theme."

"Holidays *are* good for that." Sam's glance traveled across the shelves of supplies, landing on a stack of stainless-steel bowls in graduated sizes. Hmm ... maybe so ...

She pulled them down and began experimenting. An hour later she had formed a chocolate shell in the shape of an egg, easily a foot tall. She set it in the walk-in fridge to solidify the seams and give her a good hard surface for decorating. Meanwhile, she whipped up a batch of chocolate buttercream and melted some white chocolate disks, tinting small portions in pastel colors.

"Sam? Got a minute?" Jen stood beside the curtain that separated the sales room from the kitchen. "Some people are here and said Zoë sent them by to see you."

"Are they wanting a cake?"

"That's not the impression I got. I did offer to take the details if they did. I think this is more of a quick hello. Their kids knew about the gingerbread drawing and are all over that."

"I'll be out in a sec. Just help me keep it literally to one minute, or I'll never get the giant egg done."

Jen sent her a puzzled look and a smile before leaving.

Sam washed the residue of chocolate from her hands and walked out to the crowded sales room. A tall, good-looking man and his petite wife smiled in her direction.

"You must be Samantha," he said. "Zoë at the B&B raves about your shop."

"And we have to say that the breakfast pastries have been fabulous," the wife added. "We're only in Taos one more day, so we want to get some things to take home with us."

Sam waved toward the display cases. "The scones keep well, not too fragile. Or a whole coffee cake or loaves of the quick breads. We can wrap them specially for travel."

While the wife stepped over to the case, and the two kids who appeared to be with the couple filled out entry slips for the gingerbread cottage, the husband stepped over closer to her. "Zoë also told us your husband used to be the sheriff here. I believe I've met him. Beau Cardwell, right?"

She nodded.

"I'm Steve Painter, attorney, from Albuquerque. Zoë hinted that you've also been in the law enforcement end of things and often helped local people."

Where was he going with this? She merely nodded.

"We heard the news about the current missing persons case, in fact."

"Well, yes, but I was contacted very indirectly by one of the families. The present sheriff is handling the real work. If Zoë said otherwise, I'm afraid she's a little off track on this one."

"Oh no, nothing like that," he said, with an ingratiating smile. "I just always wondered how it would be to actually solve a case like that. Afraid my work with estates and wills and such isn't nearly as exciting."

"Sometimes it's just a matter of asking enough questions. If you happen to know three families from California whose sons recently came to the area for some snowboarding, I'll take any clues I can get. Otherwise, I kind of need to ..." she gave a glance back toward the kitchen.

Steve's wife reached out and tugged at his sleeve. "Honey, help me choose something. And quit taking up this lady's time."

"Oh! Of course."

Sam gave the best smile she could muster, told Jen to slip each of the kids a chocolate chip cookie, and made a hasty exit to the kitchen.

"Important?" Becky asked.

"Just small talk. I didn't want to be rude, but people on vacation don't seem to understand that others have deadlines." She glanced up at the clock above her desk.

The giant hard-shell egg seemed firm enough when she retrieved it from the fridge, so she set to work creating a base for it, with white-chocolate grass and small colored flowers. On the egg itself, she let herself go, with freeform swirls, dots, and whimsical shapes, a chocolate-on-chocolate medley.

"Now," she said, stepping back to survey the confection, "I think a couple of hours to set up firm, and I'll be ready to take it next door."

"I love the little baby bunny you tucked there near the bottom, just as if he were hiding down in the grass," Becky said with a fond smile.

"I'm thinking of making a chocolate hammer, so they can tap the egg and break it into edible bites," Sam said. "We'll see. It may turn out to be more decorative than functional, but it seems like a cute idea."

Somehow, the hours disappeared. Jen asked if anyone wanted lunch ordered, but Sam passed and the next thing she knew it was fifteen minutes before the chocolate egg was due next door. Becky helped and they set the board into a bakery box for stability. Sam picked it up, Becky pulled the curtain aside, and Jen held the front door open as Sam balanced the delicate piece.

Ivan's eyes grew wide when he saw her approaching the bookshop. "Miss Samantha, is being your most *vkusnyy* dessert ever! The mystery club will be loving."

He pointed to the table that contained a copy of this week's book and a wide spot for the dessert, and she set it gently in place.

"It should be fun. They can crack the egg and eat big chunks of it," she said, pocketing the check he held out.

A customer stepped out from the stacks to see what the fuss was about.

"Hey, Evan! I didn't see your vehicle out front."

"I'm in my personal truck, on the way to the dentist. Riki ordered a book but she's always working until late, so I said I'd stop here and pick it up." Together, they walked over to Ivan's sales desk, where Evan pulled out cash and accepted the paperback novel Ivan put into a bag for him.

Sam spotted another book near the register and, without thinking, reached out to pick it up. *Don't Trust the Government* was the title, and the cover design depicted what looked like the inside of a 1960s bomb shelter with stacks of supplies, gas masks, and enough guns and ammo to form a small armory.

"Is for customer," Ivan commented as he handed Evan his change. "Has not come to pick up."

Sam set the book down and noticed Evan sending her a *see, I told you* look. They walked out to the sidewalk together.

"Did you—"

"Sam, I got—"

They both laughed. "Same subject?" Sam asked.

"Assuming you were going to ask about the missing young men, yes. Well, no. Nothing significant. Examining the Mustang at our local impound lot, we didn't see any evidence of a road-rage incident—no damage other than a couple of old scratches. No bullet holes, no stains like someone may have thrown food or beverage at it."

"That happens?"

"More than you would think. There was a fatal accident in Albuquerque a few years ago where someone tossed several raw eggs at a moving vehicle and blurred the driver's vision so badly they swerved into another lane. Another one where a cup of coffee flew through the driver's side window. Something like that would have splattered everywhere."

"But not in Casey Hardwick's car."

"Nope." He shifted his weight to the other foot. "If necessary, we can send the car to the state crime lab for a thorough forensic search, but at this point we don't have enough evidence to think the car is part of a crime scene. Right now, it's just an abandoned car."

Sam nodded.

"I did put in a call to California law enforcement to see if Clayton Green and his son have alibis for the days Casey and his friends were traveling. Nothing back from them yet. I wouldn't hold my breath. The pieces just don't feel right to me."

Sam thanked him but felt frustrated by the lack of leads. She'd received a text from Kelly this morning saying Casey's mother's condition had taken a turn for the worse. Where were those young men?

Chapter 20

B enjamin froze.

"Hey, man, what—" Jacob barrelled into the side of him, with Casey right behind.

Benjamin couldn't take his eyes off that pistol, the dark eye of death aimed at his face. Nancy shrank to a corner of the coat closet, pleading with her husband, staying out of the line of fire. His only coherent thought was: if she's moved aside, she believes he might really shoot. He raised his hands in submission.

"Nancy ... grab the door," Lyle said in an ominous voice as he took small sideways steps, never lowering the pistol.

As soon as he'd cleared the closet doorway, she stepped in behind him. The moment the door to the hidden room clicked shut, the opening vanished, so well concealed it was.

Nancy came out, closed the outer closet door, and stood at her husband's side. "What are we—?"

"Shush! Just shut up, all of you." As if anyone other than the wife had uttered a sound. "To the basement. Now!"

Casey led the way and as they'd always done, Jacob and Benjamin followed. The narrow hallway offered no way to spread out, no place to go other than straight ahead. When they rounded the corner and doubled back toward the basement door, Lyle ordered Nancy to make sure no one deviated. One by one, they trudged down the simple wooden steps, to the room that had become familiar to them.

At the bottom, Casey turned. "Listen, man, we won't ever tell."

Benjamin's heart sank at the expression on Lyle's face. Damn right they would never tell. The old man would now make certain of that.

Chapter 21

Sweet's Sweets was crazy on Friday, fairly quiet after the gingerbread giveaway on Saturday, and closed on Easter Sunday. Sam and Beau spent the holiday at Kelly and Scott's spacious Victorian home, watching Ana's delight over her basket of goodies and the small gingerbread cottage Sam had put together for her the day before.

Kelly had planned an open house with invites out to all the friends, and even though she woke that day with a thread of anxiety running through her—somehow related to the fact that she'd handled the carved box the night before—she welcomed everyone.

Sam took her daughter aside in the kitchen about mid-afternoon, just after Zoë and Darryl said goodbye.

"What's up?"

"Nothing. Well, I don't think it's anything," Kelly

responded while taking half the candy from Ana's basket and hiding it, hoping to avoid holiday sugar overload.

"Come on. Even Rupert noticed when he was here earlier. And Zoë almost came in to take your temperature."

"Seriously, Mom. I can't define it. I went up to the attic last night to put things away. I handled the box, but only for a couple minutes. The book of runes was lying there and I glanced at a page or two. But there wasn't … wasn't anything other than a funny feeling I got. The weather's changing—news guy said so. That must be it."

Sam gave her a sideways look. A dropping barometric pressure had never caused Kelly to be moody.

Scott came bounding in and asked if there was more potato salad. Kelly told him to check the fridge. She teased him about being full of jelly beans, he was so energetic. The whole interaction was so absolutely normal, Sam decided not to worry. If Kelly continued to feel strange, she would bring it up.

Sam carried the new bowl of potato salad into the dining room, replacing the empty one among the sumptuous buffet items. Voices from the wide front porch caught her attention, and she saw that Evan and Riki had arrived, he still in uniform. Zoë and Darryl hadn't yet made it to their car, and the foursome were chatting.

Evan spotted Sam through the window, excused himself from the group on the porch, and carried a covered bowl into the dining room.

"English trifle," he said. "Riki's specialty, made from scratch."

Sam looked at the beautiful layers in the clear bowl. It was something far too fragile to make and sell in her bakery, so she was thrilled at the new addition to the menu.

"I told Zoë and Darryl," he said. "I think they'll be staying a little longer after all. Meanwhile, I have news for you and Kelly on your missing persons."

Kelly walked in from the kitchen, carrying a refill for the platter of sliced ham. "Good news, I hope?"

"Not if you were expecting a valid suspect, apprehended and questioned, I'm afraid." He glanced toward the porch, where the others were shifting toward the front door. "Can we go in the kitchen?"

They did.

"Basically, Clayton Green told the local cops he and his son had been on a trip to Ensenada on the dates in question. The officers reached out to San Diego PD, who got in touch with Border Patrol. The alibi holds. They were on security video crossing the border into Mexico a day before your guys headed east on their trip. And US Customs scanned both of their passports coming back three days later, at the same San Diego border crossing. There's simply nothing that puts them anywhere in New Mexico, especially four hundred miles north."

Sam felt a minor letdown. When was one of their leads going to pan out? But Kelly didn't seem surprised at all.

"I had a feeling about this," Kelly said. "Something told me it wasn't going to be the answer." She gave her mother a significant look, something that told Sam not to press it, especially in front of Evan.

Voices from the dining room told them the party was back in full swing. Apparently, Zoë and Darryl had been persuaded to stay a while longer, and the newly arrived trifle was being scooped into bowls with gusto.

"I'm starved," Evan announced, pushing through the swinging door to the dining room.

Alone in the kitchen, Sam turned to Kelly. "So, what was that, a minute ago? You didn't think the lead with the Greens was going to work out. Yes, it was a bit flimsy, but what made you so sure?"

"I mentioned that I'd been near the carved box this morning … I don't know, Mom. It gave me a pretty strong feeling."

Sam saw a range of emotions cross Kelly's face.

"I can't really explain it. Just a very clear vibe that we don't yet have the right answer." She scraped the bare remains of salad from the dirty bowl, placed it in the sink, and ran water into it. "Maybe I—we—should revisit the book pretty soon."

"Now?"

Kelly glanced toward the dining room door. "We'd better go up there when we have a better chance of not being interrupted."

As if to punctuate that idea, Scott came through the doorway at that moment. "Are there more of those little rolls?"

Kelly fetched them and the two women went out to join the rest of the party, which had picked up steam again. It wasn't until dusk, when the guests had gone, the kitchen put back in order, and little Ana sacked out on the couch between her daddy and grandpa, that Kelly and Sam found their moment to sneak up to the attic.

Kelly unlocked the door and switched on the light that hung over the long trestle table. What she saw stopped her, cold.

She turned to Sam with wide eyes. "I put the book away, early this morning. I swear, it was on the shelf and the box was locked inside the cupboard. You saw—the door to this room was locked!"

Now the leather-bound volume lay open on the table. On the righthand page was the artist's rendering of the cabin in the woods.

Chapter 22

Sam arrived at Sweet's Sweets in the pre-dawn hours Monday morning. A restless night had her wide awake at three a.m. and by four she'd given up the pretense of sleep. Everything from the day before had run in an endless loop through her mind—talking Kelly down from the shock of finding the book open on the table, the disappointing but not surprising news from Evan about their theory on Casey Hardwick's potential enemy, the oddly compelling drawing of the cabin in the woods.

It was this last image that seemed most bothersome to Kelly and herself, Sam thought as she brewed coffee and sat down at her desk to evaluate today's workload. With the holiday past, the deluge of orders would be a trickle this week. Everyone had loaded up on sweets during the prior week, so it was unlikely they'd have crowds swarming the bakery cases.

She and Julio had already discussed concentrating on the savories for a few days—quiches, herb breads, cheese rolls—although there would still be customers who either didn't celebrate Easter with extra desserts or just couldn't get enough sugar in their systems. Spring break was over, kids were back in school, and life went back to normal for most.

She picked up a pad and made a quick shopping list before going online to access her favorite three wholesaler websites.

Life back to normal. The phrase stuck in her head. Except for those families whose sons had come here and not returned. Kelly had checked in with Casey's sister late yesterday afternoon, and the news was not good. Their mother's condition had worsened further, and Summer Gaines had still heard nothing from her brother.

It was still too early to call anyone on the west coast, but Sam made a note to check in with the other two families, even though she had a feeling her calls would be useless. No doubt Summer was maintaining constant contact with them.

Her supply orders placed and confirmed, she debated whether to make a light breakfast for herself now or wait for Julio to arrive and bake a quiche or two, of which she would gladly snitch a slice.

She was saved from the decision by an incoming text from Rupert.

Up early. Writing stalled. Could use company for breakfast. If you're up for it. Whenever you receive this.

She surprised him by calling him right back.

"Five-thirty and you're up?" she teased.

"It happens once in awhile. Not often, mind you." There was some rustling sound in the background, and she imagined duvet and sheets being tossed aside. There was no bright-and-early in Rupert's life. Early, maybe, but not raring to go at the same time.

"Taoseño will be open in a half hour. Want to meet there?"

"Give me forty-five. I need a shower. Mark called yesterday and, well, it didn't turn out to be a good day."

"Oh, Rupert, I'm so sorry."

"Don't get me started on that subject. I'll throw on some clothes and be there before the hour is up."

When he walked into the spacious dining room, Sam noticed the slump to his shoulders, the fact that his hair was still damp from the shower. And he was dressed all in gray again. She sighed. What more could she do, after delivering almond croissants and mocha brownies the other day?

He joined her at the small table she'd chosen, and Adeline brought coffee for both.

"I hardly got a chance to talk to you at Kelly's yesterday," she began, stirring cream into her mug. Theirs was good, but her signature blend at Sweet's Sweets was far better.

"Your daughter is such a great hostess. Good food, all the friends, and that charmer home of theirs. I just wasn't much in the mood. That's why I didn't stay long."

"Was Mark's call after you got home?"

"Yeah. I know I have to get past this, but the man just touches a nerve in me."

"It must be hard to write when you're grieving," Sam said after ordering her favorite breakfast burrito and handing the menu back to Adeline. Rupert barely gave the menu a glance before ordering the same.

"Writing? What writing? I'm staring at a blank screen all day. Half of me wants to write one of my standard gooey romances where I can control the fact that everything turns out perfectly; the other half wants to have the couple murder each other."

She smiled.

"But as my editor says, romances that don't have a happy ending just won't sell. The HEA—happily ever after—is a must."

She reached across the table and took his hand. "Happily ever after doesn't truly happen for lots of people, Rupe. Look at how many years came and went for me before Beau came along."

"But he did come along."

"Your right guy will come along someday, too."

"Okay, enough. You sound *way* too Disney," he said as the waitress delivered their burritos.

The first few bites went down in silence as Sam savored the combination of egg, potato, bacon, cheese, and green chile.

"Any news on that case you and Kelly are working on?" he finally asked, halfway through his meal.

"Nothing close to an answer yet." She told him about finding the car, about the man back in L.A. who'd once threatened one of the young men, the dead ends and false leads that were frustrating them. "I was halfway serious, you know. You should write this as a story with a good conclusion. Come up with that happy ending your editor wants, and give me some ideas for a way this could turn out well for all involved."

He shook his head ruefully, but she did notice a spark of interest. Or maybe she only *hoped* for that. She needed for her buddy to be happy again.

She let him lead the conversation, hoping that lingering over coffee would help him talk it out, but she secretly wasn't displeased when he suggested that he should go home and jot some additional plot notes. She'd given Becky two days off since the pre-holiday crush had been fairly intense, so Sam should get back and find out what needed to be baked and decorated.

They walked out to the now-full parking lot and parted with a long hug. "You take care of yourself," she admonished. "Maybe a break is in order, a quick trip somewhere."

He reminded her that he'd just had a month in the Caribbean several weeks ago. But the book deadline seemed to be looming far larger in his mind.

"You'll do it," she said, squeezing his hand. "I know you will. You've written, what, twenty books or more? You know what to do. Trust your instincts."

"I will." He climbed into his Range Rover and Sam got in her bakery van. She made a mental note to call him later in the day. This funk of his had her worried.

The bakery was busier than Sam expected when she returned. Three of the bistro tables were filled and Jen had a customer at the counter.

"Julio's back there baking quiches as fast as he can," she joked as she served up two more plates and handed the customers their wrapped cutlery.

"I'd better check in and see if I can help."

But back in the kitchen, her star baker had things under control. He'd produced more of the whole-grain alternatives and fewer of the gooey things with lots of icing, and it seemed to fit what the customers were ordering. Sam looked through the order sheets for the upcoming week and found only six birthday cakes and one bridal shower, none of which were due today.

"If you have a second, these scones are ready to go up front," Julio said, noticing she hadn't started a project yet.

"Sure thing." His cheddar scones with a hint of Old Bay seasoning were always a hit around lunch time. She picked up the tray.

Jen was wiping one of the tables. "Everyone's curious who won the drawing," she told Sam as she came back to the display case and helped fit the new tray of scones inside. "It sure generated a lot of interest. Maybe we should do that kind of thing more often?"

Sam noticed a woman standing outside, looking at the new display that featured one of their standard wedding cakes and tiered serving plates for a classic English tea. She looked up and walked inside.

"I guess the gingerbread items were already given away," she said. Her graying hair was cut in a chin-length bob, and her capris and pullover top exuded casual chic. As if she'd read Sam's thoughts she looked down at her clothing with a sigh. "Wishful thinking, dressing in summer clothing already. I hear another cold front is coming in."

"My daughter said the same thing. Spring just comes late to the mountains, doesn't it?"

The customer glanced back toward the window. "I was hoping to get another look at that little cabin you made. Was it based on a real place? I'm only asking because my best friend from high school lived in a house that looked so much like that one. Her folks lived up the ski valley road."

"Here? Taos Ski Valley?" Sam felt a shiver go down her spine.

"Cute cabin. We used to have sleepovers. Her mom was a fabulous cook, but Cindy used to talk about the weirdest things when we were in school. She and her mom got along great, but not so much with her dad. She really couldn't wait to leave for college. UNM in Albuquerque, and then she just stayed there. Married now—I was her bridesmaid and she was mine. It was that kind of friendship, but then we drifted. I only hear from her a couple times a year anymore."

"This may sound like a strange request, but do you remember the address of the cabin? I created the gingerbread piece based on a drawing of a cabin. If it's the same one, I'd love to drive by and see it."

"Oh, it looks just the same. I was up that way a few weeks ago and cruised past it. Old times, you know. I don't know an actual address but I can tell you how to get there." She picked up a napkin and drew a rough sketch, telling Sam the road names as she went.

"Do you have a minute?" Sam had a feeling she was grasping at straws, with no clue where this information would take her. "I have a picture of the drawing I worked from."

She hustled to the kitchen where she'd left her phone on the desk. Scrolling through recent photos, she quickly found the one. She'd snapped it last night at Kelly's, when they found the book lying open on the table.

"Oh my gosh, that's the one! That's the house. This looks like a watercolor. I wonder who painted it. Where on earth did you find it?"

That wasn't something Sam could exactly talk about. "Do you think your friend's parents still live there?"

"No idea, really."

"Would it be okay if I contacted her to ask that question?"

"Well, probably." But the woman backed away a step.

"Maybe if you call or text her and ask? I don't want to be too forward, but it's kind of important."

"Sure. I can send a text." She pulled out her phone and thumbed in a short message. "Just asked if they live in the same house. Is that okay?"

"Perfect." Without being obvious, Sam read sideways and memorized the number. "Thanks so much. I don't think I got your name?"

"Amanda Ross. Mandy."

"I'm Samantha Sweet. Welcome to Sweet's Sweets."

Mandy relaxed once she realized she was talking to the business owner. "I'll let you know what I hear back from Cindy. It may be a day or two. She doesn't live with her phone in her hand like so many of us do. I'll tell her about the gingerbread cabin you made. It's the kind of thing she'd get a kick out of."

"Thanks so much."

Mandy bought a cup of coffee and an oatmeal cookie, which she carried away with her. Sam began to feel a little funny about the encounter as she went back to the kitchen and started on one of the birthday cakes. The customer must have thought her request strange, for more information on the cabin. And once Sam thought hard about it, why was she asking anyway? Other than the drawing of the cabin appearing, twice now, in the leatherbound book, what connection did she actually have to the little place in the woods?

Chapter 23

Sam caught a lull in the day's business and took the opportunity to walk over to Ivan's bookshop to retrieve the board she'd used as a base for the most recent Chocoholics dessert. Ivan didn't want to keep the serving pieces and insisted it was more ecologically sound to wash and reuse them than to throw one away every week.

The bell at his door announced her, and he reached down behind his desk to pick up the two-foot-square resin board. "Giant egg was big hit," he told her. As always, he had removed the frosting-covered overlay and cleaned it up.

"I'm glad. Any ideas for this next one?"

"Big spring snowstorm coming. That can be theme?"

Sam nodded. "Maybe so. One last flourish of winter before we get into spring and summer."

He asked about the gingerbread giveaway and she told him about the big production they'd made last Saturday when customers gathered and Jen had dramatically drawn the names of two winners. One was present, and her little girl nearly bounced off the walls in excitement at being awarded the miniature chapel.

"And I guess when Jen called the other family to let them know about winning the cabin, they drove over about five minutes later to pick it up. Everyone seemed really happy for the winners. It was a great community builder."

He nodded, smiling, as he pulled books from a large carton that must have been delivered from his wholesaler. She spotted a new Nora Roberts bestseller, three J.M. Poole corgi mysteries, two books on the coming crash of the US government, and a plant guide to the wildflowers of northern New Mexico. Ivan mainly ordered according to his customers' requests, and she could see there was a lot of variety in their tastes.

She thanked him again for the idea for his next book club cake and walked outside. Glancing at the sky, she saw the telltale high, thin clouds of an approaching weather front. Ivan was the third or fourth person to mention a big storm coming in. Maybe she'd better prepare. She hurried back to the kitchen, stashed the dessert board, and paged through the forms in the order basket.

One of the birthday cakes was supposed to be delivered, and she noted that the address was up in the ski valley. Although the cake wasn't due until tomorrow, maybe it would be smart to go ahead and get it done before she potentially would have the weather to deal with. Spring storms could easily deliver eight or ten inches of heavy, wet snow in a single day.

She looked over the instructions—a standard ten-inch square layer, topped with a smaller one, decorated in a kids' zoo theme. Julio had initialed to indicate he'd baked the layers this morning, so she went to the walk-in fridge to retrieve them.

After covering the cake with green fondant, she created cartoonish animals—a zebra, giraffe, an elephant, and three pink flamingos—and a wooden-stake fence from rolled-up chocolate. An upside-down cupcake became a grass hut because … well, what kind of wild animals wouldn't want to live in a grass hut? The birthday kid was only six, and she hoped he wasn't the completely nerdy, logical type who would critique the idea to pieces.

She phoned the customer to be sure someone was home, got the directions, then loaded the cake into her bakery van. She pulled Mandy Ross's little napkin-map from the pocket in her baker's jacket where she'd stuffed it earlier this morning. The two addresses weren't exactly close together, but not far either. This would be an easy time to cruise past the little cabin that somehow seemed tied to the book of runes at Kelly's house.

Twenty minutes later she was steering up the winding ski valley road. The cake delivery was an easy one, the home being a condo near the central area where the ski lifts and parking areas converged to form the village. Ski operations were shut down now, and Sam reflected how it always seemed the case—spring break led to Easter weekend and the closure of the winter season here, then a huge dump of snow made the skiers wish the lifts had remained open an extra week or two.

She parked in the nearly empty lot and carried the cake up a short flight of wooden steps. A young woman with curly, dark hair and a baby on her hip answered the door. The sound of cartoons blasted from the interior of the condo.

"Oh my gosh, Chad is going to love this!" the woman raved when she saw the cake. She set the baby in a swing and directed Sam to place the cake box on the kitchen counter. "He's in school right now, so I'll hide it until just before the party tomorrow afternoon. Good thing you were able to drive up today." She glanced toward a sliding glass door to a back deck, eyeing the clouds. "Luckily, all the guests are kids who live right here in the neighborhood. If we get a bunch of snow, they'll just snowshoe over."

A simple life in a village that small really did hold a lot of appeal, Sam thought as she started the van and backed out. The map Mandy had sketched on the napkin lay on the passenger seat, and Sam reviewed it before taking a right turn out of the condo's parking area. Many of the roads up here didn't have signs, but she remembered it was the third turn off the main two-lane. She made that turn.

From there, Mandy had said it was three or four side roads and would be a righthand turn. The way to know she had the correct one was that there was a snaggled dead aspen tree on the left and a large boulder at the base of it.

Thank goodness it was still daylight, Sam thought as she spotted the landmarks. She'd never have found this in the dark. The one-lane side road apparently had only the one home on it, and the way was still muddy, especially in the shaded areas, but she steered carefully to the end of it. And there it was.

She wouldn't say the cabin exactly matched the picture in the book, more like a rundown version of it. The gingerbread trim was broken and missing in several places, but the wide front porch with its overhanging roofline was the same, and she could imagine it with icicles hanging in a precise row as snow would melt from the roof. A rock chimney rose squarely from the middle, and although the wood siding could use a fresh coat of stain, the basic bones of the building seemed sturdy enough.

The driveway leading to the house itself held deep ruts in the mud, and she knew better than to attempt it with her two-wheel drive vehicle. Plus, she didn't want to draw attention to herself. Then she noticed she apparently already had.

A black pickup truck with big tires and high clearance sat near a secondary structure, some kind of barn or garage. It was the only vehicle in sight, and a wiry older man with a scruff of gray chin-beard and a heavy plaid shirt stood beside it, staring at her. Damn. Her bakery van was so easily identifiable there was no way he wouldn't know exactly who was here.

She gave a faint wave, but he only scowled back. She managed a three-point turn in the roadway and headed back down the incline. She thought of Mandy's story about how her friend couldn't wait to move away. It wasn't exactly a welcoming home.

At least she'd answered for herself the question of whether the cabin from the book really did exist. Now she wished she knew how and why that might be important. The book clearly wanted her to pay attention. She would report to Kelly and maybe between them they could figure out the significance.

She steered carefully until she was back on the more heavily traveled roads, where vehicle traffic had beaten a hard path. Putting her phone on speaker, she checked in at the bakery. Nothing urgent enough that she needed to come back, Jen said. She was debating whether to run by Kelly's house or just take the more direct way home, when a text came through.

It was from Mandy Ross. Cindy called back. Yes, her parents still live in the same house. Hope that helps.

So, the old man with the black expression and the black pickup truck must be Cindy's father. No wonder the young woman couldn't wait to leave home and never go back.

Chapter 24

The door at the top of the stairs closed and a deadbolt lock clicked with finality. Casey let go with a string of obscenities and grabbed the nearest object—a book—throwing it at the closed door. The book fluttered open and barely made it to the middle step, a move so ludicrous Jacob chuckled. Casey spun on him and delivered a punch, which caught him in the shoulder.

"You bas—"

"Guys! *Guys!*" Benjamin pleaded. "We're in serious trouble here. We can't be fighting with each other."

Casey stomped to the far end of the room, flinging pillows from the couch and a lamp from an end table. He looked like he wanted to put his fist through the television screen, but stopped himself at the last second. Jacob watched with wide eyes while Benjamin's mind whirled through possibilities.

What was going on upstairs? Were the old couple planning to get rid of them, preparing a place to hide their bodies? He felt his breakfast rise into his throat.

* * *

Nancy cleared the table without a word, carrying the placemats to the back door and shaking the crumbs off, almost violently. Her mouth was set in a straight line.

"Don't you be getting all snippy with me," Lyle said from across the room, tucking the pistol into the waistband of his jeans.

"Lyle, what *were* you thinking? You *knew* the boys were right here in the kitchen. We never, *ever* open up the secret room when there's someone in the house." She turned on the hot water tap.

"I needed something out of there." Always justifying, always defending.

"Well, we're in a mess now. You couldn't quietly shut the door, make Benjamin think he'd just imagined it? You had to draw down on him?" Steam rose from the sink full of scalding water and she shut it off. "So now what? How do we get out of this?"

"No one's come looking for them. Maybe—" He stopped abruptly, cocked his head toward the front of the house.

They rushed to the living room windows.

"Shit fire, someone's coming up the road." He grabbed his heavy plaid shirt and walked out to the porch, Nancy right behind him.

Through the trees they caught a glimpse of a squarish

vehicle with bright colors. "It's a delivery van of some kind," she said. "Do *not* start anything."

"I'm not giving them a chance to walk up to this door," he said, striding down the steps to the yard. "You keep out of sight."

She backed up, closing the front door, standing well away from the window, sticking to the shadows. The van, decorated with images of bakery goods and displaying the purple logo of a shop in town, pulled up to the point where their driveway met the one-lane road. Theirs was the last property at the end of the road. Nowhere else to go beyond this. Nancy held her breath, praying Lyle would merely inform the driver that they were lost and they would quietly go away.

He stood near his truck, glaring at the other vehicle, and the driver—a woman with short, graying hair—turned the van around without entering their property.

Nancy felt the pent-up breath whoosh out of her. Thank goodness. She walked back to the kitchen and began washing the dishes. What was her hot-headed husband going to do now? And why did she always feel it was up to her to cool off these situations? Two large tears plopped into the dishwater.

Chapter 25

She'd left her own truck at Sweet's Sweets and really ought to swap it for the bakery van, so she headed in that direction. But the turnoff to Kelly's appealed more than going back to work. Jen had assured her everything was under control. She might as well take the time for a cup of tea with her daughter.

Kelly stood at the kitchen counter, chopping onions. "I'm making green chile stew tonight. Figured if the temp is dropping, and this big storm is coming in, I might as well take advantage of one last chance to cook hearty before summer gets here."

"Good point. Another reason I'd better leave the van at the bakery and take my truck home."

Kelly laughed. "Just watch. The so-called *huge* storm will turn out to be nothing at all and we'll be putting the stew in the freezer for another time."

"It's definitely getting colder out. I think you're safe. Mind if I put on the tea kettle?"

"I was just going to suggest it. As soon as I get all these ingredients into the big pot, all I have to do is watch it simmer."

"I had a delivery up in the ski valley just now, and I drove up to that cabin."

"Is it adorably picturesque?"

"Well, not exactly. I mean, it's not bad, just not a fairytale structure." Sam relayed what she'd observed, including the grumpy looking man and the black truck. "I've been thinking about the daughter who left. For some reason—probably the book of runes—I still feel drawn to that place. It keeps coming back into my consciousness. Does that sound weird?"

"Only a little. But not really. I've seen that image too, and it really does stick with you somehow." She added the onions to the cubed pork that was already browning in the stewpot. "So, call the daughter. You'll think of some way to bring up the subject."

"She already knows I've been asking about the house. The bakery customer who gave me the directions has been in touch with her."

While Kelly added tomatoes, green chile, broth, and seasonings to her recipe, Sam texted Mandy, the customer from the bakery. Within a minute, she'd received a response. Sure, Cindy had mentioned that she'd love to know more about this watercolor of the cabin where she grew up. She included her friend's phone number. It was at least a conversation opener.

"I'm just one of those people who believes that the

universe delivers certain messages to us for a reason," Cindy said, once Sam had introduced herself and Kelly over the speaker phone. "The fact that you found that picture in a book, then created a gingerbread replica, then my friend saw that in your shop window, and told you what a match it was … Wow. I'm impressed."

"Mandy told me your parents still live there. I was up in the ski valley this afternoon for a delivery and I drove up to the end of the road. Didn't approach the cabin or anything, since I thought they might find that a little intrusive."

There was a snort from the other end. "My dad finds everything intrusive. Mom … well, she would have probably welcomed the company. She misses female company. I realize that, but I just cannot go back. She rarely gets to Albuquerque on her own, but once in a while we meet up in Taos."

"Mandy said there was some kind of split with your parents. That's too bad."

"Oh yeah. And if you've got a few hours, I can tell you all about it."

"You don't have to—I mean, I'm sure it's very personal."

Cindy sighed. "My dad and I, well, we just never were on the same wavelength. The thing I just said about seeing a sign from the universe. He'd have given me a two-hour lecture on that. He has faith in *nothing*. He wasn't always like that. When I was a kid, we went camping and fishing, and I loved long walks in the forest with both my parents. But he started listening to these conspiracy theory nuts. Everything and everyone is out to get you. Gotta prepare for the coming apocalypse. The paranoia became the overriding feeling in our house."

Sam and Kelly had carried the phone to the kitchen table and sat down with their tea.

"I tried to convince Dad to get help. No way was he listening to some smart-mouth teenage girl. I begged Mom to get him some help, but he'd talk to her the same way."

"And she just put up with it?"

"What choice did she have? Mom grew up in the '50s, in a family where the women cared for their homes and their men. The man brought in the money so he was the one who said how things would go. She married him straight out of high school and never had more than a simple clerking job, no career. And I have to say, he did provide well enough for us. He worked for the Forest Service, until he started getting the idea that the government was spying on everybody. Due to an injury, he was able to retire a few years early with a disability income, and he filled in the gaps by selling firewood, recycling scrap metal, that kind of thing. He'd paid off the land early, built the cabin himself, so we had very few bills."

"You and your mom have stayed close, though. That's good."

"It is. I need to know she's safe, so I encourage her to talk. If I ever get the sense that she's in any danger, I don't care what happens, my husband and I will drive right up there and get her out."

"You think your dad would harm her?"

"No. Well, probably not. She is a very devoted wife and pretty much his one ally in this world. Well, outside of those survivalist nuts he's started hanging out with."

"Up here? Around Taos?"

"There are some. I don't have names, but I know there are two or three guys who all compare notes on what they'll do when the government comes after their homes and their guns." Cindy paused and took a deep breath. "Don't get me wrong. I don't think they're raving lunatics. Just a few old men who've gotten a little close to the edge."

Evan—or was it Beau—had mentioned being aware of them. Sam remembered the somewhat radical books she'd seen at Ivan's. "I feel kind of sorry for your mother," Kelly said.

"Me too. Her life right now doesn't seem very happy, but she doesn't have a clue what she would do on her own. I just do my best to keep in touch with her, let her know I'm here for her if it gets so bad she just can't stand it anymore. But then she doesn't like to hear me talk that way, to acknowledge that things aren't perfect for her. So, mostly we talk about my kids or the weather or I fill her in on what we're doing in my household."

"I'm so sorry," Sam said. "I hope our calling didn't bring you down. It sounds like you've got your life and your situation figured out."

That elicited a laugh. "I like to think so. We're good. It's all good. And thanks for the therapy session. I guess I need to talk it out sometimes. It's just the nature of how our traumatic experiences affect us."

They ended the call. "Our traumatic experiences?" Kelly said, raising an eyebrow. "She didn't elaborate on any specific thing that sounded traumatic, but there must have been huge arguments. Maybe she felt as though she was running for her own life when she left that household."

"I hadn't thought of that," Sam admitted. She drained her tea mug and set it down. "Interesting, how the use of one phrase takes the meaning of the conversation down a whole new path."

A gust of wind rattled the kitchen window and the back door shook a little.

"I gotta get going," she said, reaching for her coat, hanging beside the back door. "The storm is moving in quicker than I thought it would."

Chapter 26

Benjamin paced the length of the basement room, went into the adjoining bathroom, paced back out again. Casey had acted like a caged animal during the first hour they were down here, but eventually he'd crashed to the sofa, where Jacob was already fiddling with the video game controller. Clueless, Benjamin thought. Did they not understand how precarious their position was?

His blue nylon duffle bag came thumping down the flight of stairs, stopping him in his tracks. There stood Lyle at the top, the pistol in his right hand, about to toss another duffle with his left. Behind him, Nancy stood with a tray in her hands. Benjamin hadn't even heard the deadbolt unlock.

"None of you move!" Lyle shouted as all three guys jumped to their feet and stared up at him. Three sleeping bags tumbled down, followed by two more duffles, basically all the luggage they'd brought with them. "My wife is leaving you some food, here on the landing."

"What are you going to do with us?" Casey demanded. "You can't keep us prisoner."

Lyle didn't respond. He backed off just enough for Nancy to gingerly set the food tray down, then he closed and locked the door again.

"What the f—"

"Casey! Stop it! We need to think clearly, not just sit down here and rant."

Benjamin walked up and picked up the food tray. It held six sandwiches, two large bags of chips, a glass jug of iced tea, and three plastic cups. They would need nourishment, if his idea were to work. He handed out sandwiches.

* * *

"Honey, listen. Just stop and think. This can't go on forever," Nancy pleaded as she carried the tray and empty iced tea jug back to the kitchen that night. "They were so exhausted I was able to tiptoe down there, but we can't keep drugging their food to keep them quiet. What if someone does come around, looking for them? They've been gone from home for days now. Someone will report them missing."

Lyle pulled her into a hug. "Trust me. I'm coming up with a plan."

The whole thing had seemed so harmless at first. Inviting the lost kids in for the night, planning to help them find their actual accommodations the next day. At least that's what she thought they would do. Then Lyle had to go and take their car away. That's when it all started to go wrong.

She had to admit, she'd loved having young people around again, and when the weather turned and the mud got so thick, well, it was harmless enough to string them along, keep feeding them, pretend to herself that she had a little family again.

Lyle backed away from the embrace, heading now for the front door. What was he going to do? It scared her a little, thinking about what he might be capable of.

Chapter 27

Wind whistled through some tiny airspace at one of the windows. When had that started happening? Sam didn't recall this particular sound. Must be a spot where the air movement had to come from one particular direction in order to create a sound. Kind of like when you pursed your lips one way and got nothing but a quiet little *whiii* and then shifted a little something and came out with a loud whistle. And what was she doing, thinking of this at ... she rolled over to look at the clock ... 2:51 in the morning?

She got up and pulled her thick fleece robe over her shoulders as she walked toward the bedroom window. Snow whirled past, driven in a vortex somehow caused by the slant of the roofline, the log walls, the nearby trees ... she wasn't sure. Only that it would be a miserable night to be outside. She thought of Beau's years as sheriff, when he'd been forced out on nights like this. At times, he still missed the job. At times like *this*, she was thankful to have him breathing quietly in their bed, safe and warm.

She thought of the three missing young men. Where were they now?

Surely, they had found shelter and warmth. These were city kids, accustomed to Southern California's weather, beaches, palm trees. They'd found alternate accommodations. Somehow.

She turned away from the window and crawled back under the covers. Dwelling on a set of complete unknowns would not serve anyone. She pulled the heavy comforter over her shoulders and concentrated on sleep, as the whistling wind finally quieted.

Chapter 28

Nancy heard the wind in the night. A tree near the house brushed the roofline repeatedly, creaking as the trunk rubbed against the eaves. Trimming it was a project they needed to tend to this summer. The boys were asleep in the basement—she'd checked—and Lyle lay beside her, asleep now. But their conversation as they got ready for bed weighed on her, the words now running in a loop in her head.

"This situation can't go on forever, honey. What are we going to do?"

He rinsed his mouth and put his toothbrush in the holder. "I got a plan, Nance. Don't fret. I can load 'em in my truck when they're real sleepy, take 'em somewhere in the middle of town, dump 'em off. They'll wake up and have no idea where they've been all this time. No way to pin anything on us. Mainly, they'll be happy as hell to get back to California."

"Will they? Let the whole thing drop?"

"We'll do it tomorrow. Storm will pass through in twenty-four hours and we'll get 'em to town tomorrow night."

Now, she pushed the quilt aside to dissipate the heat that had built up around her body. What if Lyle's plan went awry? Aside from the physical feat of getting each of these three grown men transferred from the basement to the truck—all hundred-fifty pounds of her husband—how could he count on the boys not running straight to the police with their story?

She'd seen the fury on his face when the boys got a look at the hidden room. He guarded that secret with his life. Even his closest anti-government comrades had never seen it. Many of them had built similar hidey-holes on their property, but Lyle was one who'd never shared the details about his space. Now, three outsiders knew about it, could pinpoint it to the authorities if law enforcement staged a raid on the cabin. She'd read every bit of that in Lyle's expression. It would be far simpler to drag the boys deep into the forest, kill them, and leave their bodies for the coyotes and buzzards to deal with. He'd find a place where no one could connect him to the crime, even if the bodies were ever found.

Her throat swelled and she choked back a sob. How had their lives taken such a nasty turn?

* * *

"Casey. Casey!" Benjamin shook his friend's shoulder

and watched him struggle to climb to consciousness.

"Hey, man. Wake up. We gotta get out of here."

"What time is it? How long have we been here?"

"No idea. All our phones are gone. You're the guy with the smartwatch."

Casey raised his arm futilely. "Which died at least two days ago. I couldn't find my charger." He sat up and rubbed vigorously at his eyes. Jacob was lying on the floor nearby, tangled in his sleeping bag, beginning to stir.

"I think they drugged us. Something in the food," Casey said.

"You think? It started with the hot chocolate, right after we spotted that hidden space, whatever *that* was all about." Benjamin remembered feeling wary about the sandwiches but they'd been so hungry, and he hadn't been able to stop either of the others from attacking the food. He'd eaten the bare minimum to stave off his own hunger. "Told you."

He nudged Jacob into wakefulness and gathered the others close by, keeping his voice low. "I've been thinking about this. I don't know where we are, but anyplace is better than this cabin with this nutcase. While you guys were asleep, I searched the room and gathered some stuff." He held up a matchbook with four matches and a bobby pin. "Found these in the back of a drawer in the bathroom."

Casey stared at him as though he'd sprouted wings or something.

"Hey, I spent a couple years in scouting, went camping a bit. Did either of you?"

Both shook their heads.

"Okay then. I think I can get us out. Go through your stuff and show me what resources we can pull together."

Dumping the duffle bags netted an assortment of clothing, a minimal toiletry kit for each of them, two phone chargers, a copy of *Hustler* (Casey's, of course), a packet of gummy worms and one of tortilla chips (Jacob's, naturally). Benjamin began rifling through the shaving kits to see what could be useful.

"Put on several layers of clothes," he instructed. "Your warmest stuff, except save your outer jackets until we get outside. Don't want to start sweating in here."

Casey gave him a look: *whatever.* Jacob started to open the tortilla chips.

"Save those. We don't know how long it'll be until we get food again." Benjamin could tell they both thought there was probably a McDonald's just at the bottom of the hill. He was pretty sure that was not the case. From the gear in front of him, he retrieved anything sharp—some nail scissors and two disposable razors—plus the laces from two pairs of boots and the phone charger cords. He stuffed everything into his pockets.

"Chargers, really?"

"They have wire in them. Anything that can be tied in a knot could come in handy."

"If you say so." Casey went back to choosing between two pairs of jeans.

The first challenge, of course, would be to pick the lock on the basement door, then to get out of the house without Lyle hearing them. Benjamin climbed the stairs, staying to the outside edges of each step, in case one of them creaked. He had the bobby pin in hand. A girl had once told him it was the way she routinely broke into her brother's bedroom to use his computer.

But the deadbolt lock wasn't the same as that on a

standard bedroom doorknob. The pin wouldn't handle the lock's tumblers alone. He'd seen a video once on the art of picking locks, and all he knew was that it required at least two sturdy picks and a lot of experience. He grabbed the knob in frustration.

It turned. The door came open, just an inch.

Whoa. He stared, trying to piece together his good luck. He'd tried it last night after the food was delivered and the thing was securely locked. Then he remembered, a vague notion that Nancy had checked on them after she believed they were asleep. Yes—the food tray was gone. She had come at least as far as the landing. And she must have forgotten to twist the deadbolt or the doorknob lock.

Did she forget? Or had she purposely given them a means of escape?

He didn't have time to analyze it now. They just needed out!

He peered through the narrow crack by the doorjamb. The house was dark and quiet, with only the faint glow of something—maybe a nightlight in another room—to show the outline where the wall divided the living room from the kitchen. He pushed the door closed and hurried to the others, whispering instructions.

"It's dark, but I have no idea how long until daybreak. We have to hurry!" He patted his pockets to be sure he'd taken what he wanted, donned the outer shell he'd brought for snowboarding, and made sure the others did the same.

"Be absolutely quiet until we're outside. Guys, we *cannot* let Lyle catch us." He could only hope Casey, the normal ringleader of the group, would listen to him.

Benjamin led the way, signaling the others to halt as soon as they were out of the basement. He gently drew the door closed. Anything to buy them a few extra minutes, once the old couple were awake. He risked crossing the hallway to take a quick look into the kitchen. The digital numbers on the microwave showed 2:53. Excellent. They had several hours before anyone was likely to be awake.

He tiptoed back to the others and led the way to the front door, trying to remember whether it had a squeak. He undid the locks and pulled it open as little as necessary to slip through, signaled to Casey to come next, Jacob to close the door behind them. They stepped to the edge of the porch, where their boots immediately dipped into six inches of fresh snow.

The world in front of them was nothing but a thick, disorienting white.

Chapter 29

Beau woke Sam with a trail of kisses down her neck and over her left shoulder. If one had to be awakened by someone, this was definitely her favorite way for it to happen. Other than their bodies fitting together, the only thing she noticed was that the wind had stopped. It wasn't until later, as they stepped into the shower together, that she got a glance at the clock and saw it was a little after six.

Beau washed, dried, and dressed first, heading downstairs to make the coffee while she took her time shampooing and drying her hair.

"I'd guess eight inches, still coming down," he said, staring out the kitchen window as Sam poured her coffee. "They said on the radio that it's even more in the higher elevations."

Sam thought of the isolated cabin in the woods, until

her attention was drawn back home. Both dogs seemed eager to go out, and Beau opened the front door for them, laughing as they hesitated only a fraction of a second before lunging into snow that came nearly to their bellies. They quickly finished their business and headed for the porch again. Sam noticed ice balls clinging to their fur.

"That's some wet snow. Don't let them back in unless you're ready with a towel," she said.

"I heard the county plow out on the road. Imagine we can get ourselves down the length of our driveway." He gathered two old towels and tended to the dogs, while Sam scooped kibble into their bowls in the kitchen.

Both of their vehicles were high clearance and four-wheel-drive, so it shouldn't be a problem. Sam called her employees to say that anyone who felt uneasy driving to the bakery could stay home until their pathway was clear. She had run the business by herself for the first few months and could do it again for one morning. Normally, a spring snow like this would melt quickly. Of course, it didn't appear the storm was quite finished yet, and there was no sign of sunshine yet.

A delayed opening wasn't going to hurt the bakery business on a day like this, so she made cinnamon toast at home for the two of them, and whipped up a couple of scrambled eggs for Beau.

"I'll make the first run," he said, "pack down a track so you can get out to the road."

They put on coats and picked up a broom and shovel, clearing a path down the steps and out to the vehicles. As their trucks warmed up, Sam swept her windshield clear. Beau steered his truck slowly toward the county road, letting the wide tires make a set of tracks, then turned around and widened the path a bit more for Sam. She blew him a kiss as she shifted into four-wheel-drive and made her way out.

The kitchen at Sweet's Sweets felt chilly, but the atmosphere quickly warmed as she fired up the oven and switched on lights. Out front, she noticed the landlord's plowing service had not come yet, and there were no tracks in the smooth white surface of the parking lot. She wouldn't bother to turn out the night lights until she had something to offer for sale.

With the tubs of dry ingredients that Julio usually blended ahead, she stirred in the eggs, oil, and milk for muffin batter, added blueberries to two dozen, cranberries and orange zest to another dozen, and whipped up oat bran to make another batch. Twenty minutes later, warm muffin scent filled the air, and she had the scones rolled out and ready to bake.

By the time the plow showed up to clear the parking lot, the bakery was operational for anyone who was up for a quick breakfast, and the first vehicle she spotted was Sheriff Evan. She signaled him with an uplifted coffee mug and he got out of his cruiser.

"Just dropped Riki off, although it doesn't look like her customers are exactly racing down here," he said. "That's okay. She has a hard time finding a spare minute to sweep up dog hair and replenish supplies. She's always glad for a little break between grooming jobs."

"I'll set aside a couple of muffins for her," Sam said. "You can carry them over before you leave."

He accepted a mug of coffee and two blueberry muffins and sat down at one of the little tables. "I hear there's a lot of snow up in Taos Ski Valley. You know, it kind of gets a 'bowl' effect when the wind blows, really can collect up there, feet deep."

"Is there any word—?" He shook his head. They were both thinking the same thing.

"I called the woman, the one who reported her brother missing. She hasn't heard anything at all, and neither have the other two families."

"Good thing she's acting as a sort of liaison with them, or you'd be getting three times the number of calls."

He shook his head sadly, "I wouldn't mind, really. If one of those calls brought some kind of lead, it'd be worth the interruption."

"Nothing coming in locally? The news coverage has been good, the pleas for information."

"Nothing with a positive ID. There are always sightings, and we've checked them all. And, of course, the TSV police are on alert as well. There hasn't been so much as a footprint." He stared out the front windows. "Of course, that's really saying something after a snowfall like this one."

Sam felt her eyes well up. She and Kelly had been really hoping for positive news before this.

"We'll get a lead soon, Sam. They have to be out there somewhere. Three people don't just vanish without a trace. We're still evaluating the evidence from the car, too."

She nodded. "I know you'll find them." She set two muffins in a bakery bag and filled a takeout cup with her signature blend coffee for Riki before he left.

His cruiser had barely left the lot when Jen pulled up, and Sam noticed more traffic on the street. The workday was about to begin, snow or no snow.

Chapter 30

The one thing they had going for them, when it came to dodging Lyle and the inevitable retribution, was the wind. At least Benjamin hoped so. Their first step off the cabin's front porch had put them up to their knees in heavy snow. There was no way they could go anywhere without leaving an obvious trail.

They were three inexperienced guys, with no resources other than a few strings, tiny scissors, and a matchbook, against a man familiar with the terrain and surrounding area. An armed man. It was almost laughable. He didn't dare think about it.

Hopefully, the wind would soon obscure their tracks.

One thing they impressed upon the kids at Scout camp was that if they were ever lost they should head down hill. Down would lead to a river or stream. Down normally led to roads. Uphill only led deeper into the woods. The challenge here was in figuring out which way was down.

The cabin sat in a very small clearing with trees all around. He remembered the driveway being a bit of a climb from the road, but where was the driveway? Everything in his vision was white—the air, the ground, the tree branches, even the tree trunks. Snow swirled everywhere. He could only rely on gravity, feeling whether his steps were leading up or down. Without visual clues, even the slightest rise in the ground might fake him out, make him think he should go the other direction.

The others were no help. Jacob had forgotten his gloves and kept complaining that his hands were cold. Keeping them in his pockets helped, but then his balance was off—he'd fallen twice before they were far from the cabin. And Casey didn't have a hat or goggles. The hood of his jacket kept blowing backward, exposing him to potentially life-threatening heat loss.

Benjamin felt the weight of responsibility. It would be up to him to get them out of here. He paid attention to his feet and kept them angled downward. Until he ran smack into the trunk of a tree. At least they were out of the clearing where Lyle was likely to spot them.

Chapter 31

Julio and Becky were at work in the kitchen thirty minutes later, she having offered him a ride in an actual car instead of his having to go with his normal Harley. They'd used the arrangement several times over the winter months and it worked out well for all. Sam had been dwelling on what Evan said earlier, about the forensic tests on the Mustang. She couldn't shake the feeling that a valuable clue existed there, so she left the cake orders in Becky's capable hands and headed for the sheriff's office.

Evan was out, and the squad room was empty except for Rico, a deputy she'd worked with often.

"It's a mess out there," he said, staring at a computer screen while lines of numbers flashed across the screen. "People who have no clue how to drive in snow are out on the road and we're responding to collisions and stranded drivers who managed to slide off the highway."

"What's this?" Sam asked with a nod at the screen.

"You had one of your intuitions, didn't you?" he said with a smile. "We found a fingerprint in the Mustang from that missing persons case."

She hated admitting just how strong the feeling had been earlier, so she didn't.

"And this program is running the print through some databases and will find a match?"

"*Might* find a match." He gave a sigh. "It's iffy and it takes forever, and all I have available to me is the county records. If we're looking for someone whose prints are only in a federal database—say, if they served in the armed forces but were never printed elsewhere—that takes a whole other level of search that I can't perform."

"Oh. Doesn't sound too promising. But what if the print is from someone in California?" She was thinking of the man who'd previously owned the car, even though it seemed he'd been ruled out as a suspect.

"We'd have to send it higher up for that too."

"Where in the car was the print found?"

"Now, that is your best question yet. It was on the key." He looked at her expectantly, waiting for her to put it together.

"And for the print to show on the key, it means that person handled it after Casey Hardwick."

"We're fairly sure the print isn't Casey's because there are matching prints all over the place, from the door handles to the radio buttons to the gearshift, and this one's different. Same with prints from the other two boys. Front seat and back, there are complete prints from three individuals. This is not from any of them."

Sam bit her lower lip, thinking hard. "Somebody probably moved the car after Casey last drove it and they handled the key. But wouldn't their prints also be on the steering wheel and gearshift?"

"Unless they were smart enough to wipe those off. A lot of the prints in those areas were blurred."

"But they didn't think about the key."

"We've talked this out endlessly here in the department. Why was the key in the car, right? Because whoever parked it at the motel probably hoped it would be an easy target and get stolen, taken out of state, or otherwise just vanish. Of course, that's speculation. But it's one detail we haven't shared with the press, the fact the key was in the car."

"So, how long will it take to compare the digitized print with the county records? Are there really that many?"

"More than you would think. Every person ever booked through our department or the police departments throughout the county. That's every DWI, every petty theft, and who knows what else. If you're wanting to watch the whole process, I'm fine with having the company, but you'd better pull up a chair."

She laughed and patted his shoulder. "No thanks. Sounds like it will be hours. But tell Evan I'd like to know how it goes."

Sam was getting into her truck when Kelly called.

Chapter 32

What were we thinking, leaving in the dark? In the adrenaline rush to leave the cabin and simply get away, Ben realized they hadn't thought through the consequences. He stared at their white-gray surroundings, the huge pines laden with snow, the patches where the ground showed through, the drifts where he'd suddenly be in snow up to his knees. They had no clue where they were.

In his scouting days, he would have been carrying a pack with a compass and a pocket knife, some food and basic necessities. They would have studied a map, had at least a rudimentary sense of direction in mind. There was always an adult with them. For a brief moment he caught himself yearning for his mother, a feeling he hadn't truly experienced since he was ten. Okay, maybe twelve. She would know what to do. She was a take-charge lady. He blinked and sniffed away those thoughts.

Stop it. You were a little kid. Of course there was always an adult there. Now you're the adult, and you're the most knowledgeable one in this bunch. Act like it.

At least the wind had died down and the temperature wasn't sub-zero. Things could be worse.

He looked at the other guys. Jacob was lagging behind, awkwardly walking along with his bare hands tucked under his armpits, stumbling every time his feet hit uneven ground. Casey's hood was at least staying in place now, but his face looked chapped and the tip of his nose was an ominous white. He paused to let them catch up, scanning the sky.

The sun looked milky behind the cloud layer. The snowflakes were smaller now, not the dollar-sized sticky ones that had piled upon everything during the night.

"Where's the road?" Casey's voice startled him, close behind.

"Well, that way is east," Benjamin said, pointing in the direction of the sun. "So, we're facing south."

"Doesn't answer my question, dork."

Benjamin felt himself hovering near the edge. "I don't *know* where the road is! Do you?"

Jacob stood ten feet away, listening. "True, man. You drove us here."

Casey whirled. "And you left the map and directions behind." He took an aggressive step toward Jacob.

"Guys! Stop this!" Benjamin could see the whole situation devolving into chaos that would end with the three of them dead. "There's no point. Right now, we just gotta get out of here. Do either of you have an idea which way it is to town?"

"Taos is south of the ski valley," Casey said, stating the obvious. There was also a 13,000 foot mountain peak between the two.

Jacob merely waved an arm vaguely uphill from where they stood. Benjamin knew that wasn't correct. Plus, they couldn't risk heading back toward the cabin and having Lyle catch them. So, no help from the guys.

He debated about clearing a spot and building a little fire, to use one of their precious matches. But every twig and pine needle was soggy wet, and what would they do with a fire anyway? It might be different if they'd thought to bring some kind of vessel. Even a tin cup would work to melt snow, heat the water, have something warm to drink. But that wasn't an option.

Better to just keep moving while they had daylight. He listened intently, hoping to catch the sounds of vehicles on roads. Nothing. Even the birds, it seemed, were hunkered down in the wake of the storm. He swallowed his despair and pointed the way downhill.

Chapter 33

"What's up, Kel?" Sam started her truck and let the engine idle so it would warm up enough to turn on the heater.

"Summer Gaines called me again. She says Lisa Packard is on her way up."

Sam's mind went blank for a second.

"Benjamin Packard's mother. Summer says she flew into Albuquerque on the earliest flight this morning and was in the process of changing her rental car to something with all wheel drive. She'll probably be here before noon."

"Think I should warn Evan? She'll probably head for his office first."

"Might be a good idea."

Sam told Kelly about the fingerprint search Rico was doing.

"So you've got an excuse to go back and hang around when Lisa shows up, eavesdrop on the conversation."

Sam doubted the sheriff needed her input when it came to the parents of the missing young men. She told Kelly she would be happy enough to let her text Evan with the information. She drove back to the bakery, glad to see high piles of snow where the parking lot and back alley had been plowed.

It was 11:57 on the dot when Sam received a text from Evan. **Mom of one of the missing kids is here. Want to sit in?**

Well, okay, she was secretly glad for the invite. She shed her baker's jacket and fluffed her hair a little before heading to the sheriff's department, two blocks away. Kelly was just pulling into the visitor parking area, and Sam suspected her daughter was actually the one who'd convinced Evan to include them.

When they walked in, Evan introduced Sam as a former deputy who'd offered to help on the case, while her daughter Kelly was a friend of the Hardwick family. Sam reminded her they'd spoken on the phone. Lisa Packard wore a stiff gabardine pantsuit and an equally stiff blonde pageboy haircut that didn't move when she nodded. She greeted them with a firm handshake.

"I'm a bottom-line kind of person," she said, the moment they were all seated in front of Evan's desk. "So I'll get right to it. Over the past week, I've become closer than I would have imagined to the Hardwick family and to Jacob Winters' mother. I'm here to get Casey Hardwick home as quickly as possible to see his mother before she passes. How are we going to accomplish that, Sheriff?"

"I appreciate that, ma'am, and I want to assure you that we're doing all we—"

"I'm sure you think so," Lisa interrupted. "But the bottom line is that Casey's mother doesn't have long."

He drew himself up a little straighter in his chair. "I'm—we *all*—are very sorry to hear that. We've been made aware of their situation—"

Lisa tutted, letting him know his good intentions were not what she was looking for.

Sam turned in her chair to face the woman directly. "Lisa, please. Work with us here. The sheriff, and all of us, have followed a number of leads. The department is reviewing the little bit of forensic evidence that's been recovered ... there just hasn't been a lot to go on."

"I should have never let Benjamin come to this ... this backwater town."

"Wait a minute!" Kelly took over. "I don't know if you thought you would walk in here and someone would be able to take you straight to your son, but that's not how it goes. Please just calm down a little."

Evan placed his hands flat on his desk. "We all need to calm down a little. This isn't the big city, that's true. We don't have the same resources. It doesn't mean we care any less or will do any less to solve whatever comes our way. We want your son and his friends found, safe and unharmed, every bit as much as you do."

Lisa defrosted by quite a bit. "Sorry. This has been such an emotional time—for all of us. The Hardwick family is especially hard-hit, but Jacob's parents are equally devastated. If they'd had the means, they would have been here too. We're all really at a loss for what to do."

As are we, Sam thought privately.

"It's wonderful that your three families have pulled together," Kelly said. "Really, Summer has had so much good to say about everyone's support and cooperation."

Lisa almost smiled. "As I said, I'm always looking for the bottom line. What do you have that I can take back to the families? Any information would be helpful."

Evan pulled out the file and went through the list of interviews, how he'd determined that the boys never arrived at their vacation rental, and what they'd done when the car had been found several towns away.

"Did Casey's family say anything about someone else who might have hitched a ride with the three boys?" he asked. "Another person who would have a reason to be in the car with them?"

She shook her head, confirming what Kelly had already asked Summer.

He paged through to other interviews and shared basic information with Lisa. Through the glass window that faced the squad room, Sam caught movement. Rico was on his feet, heading toward Evan's private office. He tapped once and opened the door.

"Sheriff, I've got a result."

"Sam, can you go check that out?" In other words, find out if it's something we should share with the visitor.

She stood and followed Rico to his desk. He pulled up an extra chair, setting it so she could see his computer screen, which at the moment contained only a blue background filled with boxes of words and numbers.

"The print belongs to a Lyle Bolton. Last known address is 14 Chipmunk Lane, Taos Ski Valley."

Sam knew that address. "Do you have a picture of him?"

The photo was probably two decades old. The man's hair was dark, his face less wrinkled, but Sam felt sure it was the same man she'd seen near the black pickup truck, the one who stared as she approached the property.

Rico noticed her reaction. "You've seen him around?"

"What's he in the system for?"

"Disturbing the peace. It was nearly twenty years ago—wow, can that be?" He paused with his own thoughts for a minute. "Anyway, yeah, I remember this one. There was some anti-government protest down at the old city hall—before they built the new building. I don't remember the name of the group or what their gripe was. It's probably in the report somewhere, if we still have it. Bunch of people yelling about their rights and how the government was taking everything away. Couple of them waved rifles in the air. Unloaded, it turned out. They were just making a point."

Sam pictured scenes from old newsreels. "Did they all get detained?"

"Just the ones who stepped over the line. Including Bolton. He came unglued and threw a rock at a deputy. That was me. I was so rookie at the time I didn't know what to do. Beau stepped right up and cuffed the guy before he knew what was happening. Screamed all the way down here, until we got inside the building. He just wanted the news cameras to hear him shouting those slogans, I suppose."

"He was booked?"

"Yeah. Disturbing the peace, threatening a law officer with intent of bodily harm. I suppose the rock would have raised a welt, except it missed me." He gave a wry grin. "But that's how his prints got into the system. He's probably still on a couple of those watch lists, in case he should ever start something even more serious."

Sam shifted in her seat, reading the lines on the screen.

"Sam? I repeat—you've seen this guy around?"

"Yes, pretty sure. I drove up that direction recently, past the address you have here, and I'm fairly certain the man I saw in front of the house was him. Gray now, kind of skinny. But tough looking. He sure stared me down. I turned around without entering the property and drove away."

"What led you to go up there in the first place?"

A drawing in a book? Talking with his estranged daughter? Those didn't seem like the kinds of answers he expected.

"A customer came in the bakery and we got into this roundabout conversation involving a gingerbread house I'd made. A good friend from her school days grew up in that cabin in the ski valley. I was curious to see what it looked like."

"That's it? Nothing to do with the case you've been helping us with?"

She had to think a long moment. Did he really need the explanation about the drawing in the magic book? No. But she wanted to be truthful. "Well, now I'm beginning to wonder. At the time, I swear it was just an interest in seeing what the cabin looked like."

"And now that we can place Bolton in the car that belonged to the missing boys?"

"That surprises me. I genuinely don't know how to connect them."

Chapter 34

Evan's door opened, the meeting clearly over. He seemed to be reassuring Lisa Packard that he was personally following all the leads, as he suggested she go on over to her hotel and check in. He would be in touch.

"I need to get home anyway," Kelly said. "I'll walk with you out to the parking lot."

Evan watched them leave the squad room then sauntered over. Rico and Sam filled him in on the fingerprint connect and the lead to Lyle Bolton.

"I need to get out there and talk to this guy," he told them. "Put out a radio call for some backup. It's not going to be a warm welcome, I imagine."

Rico left to speak with the dispatcher, but he was back in under a minute. "All units are tied up, Sheriff. Mostly traffic stuff."

"Okay. Hate to leave the squad room completely empty, but you'll need to come. Sam, you too, if you can. You know where the place is."

The two law enforcement men geared up, sidearms and equipment belts in place. Evan had a snapshot of the red Mustang handy in the inside pocket of his coat. He loaned Sam a jacket with department insignia.

"So, am I being officially deputized again?" she asked with a little smile.

"Only if you want to be. I just figured this would be a warmer coat than what you were wearing when you came in, and it gives you a little official cred. But I don't expect you to say or do anything. Let me do the talking."

She was more than happy to comply with that request. She rode with Evan in the front seat of the cruiser that used to belong to Beau, a little nagging nostalgia tugging at her. Rico followed in his patrol vehicle. Both SUVs were ready in case the roads higher up the mountain hadn't been cleared yet.

Sam pointed out the turns she taken the other day. "Looks like the county or somebody got out early with a plow." She pointed out the landmark she'd used to find Chipmunk Lane, since there was no road sign to mark it. "The cabin is at the very end of this, maybe a quarter mile, and it sits at the point where the road dead-ends. The driveway to the cabin slants uphill at a pretty good angle."

Evan nodded and patted the dashboard. "This puppy's pretty good in the snow, but we'll walk in if we need to."

The snow was close to eight inches deep, Sam guessed, but Evan was right. He put the cruiser in low gear and powered his way up the driveway until he came to the clearing in front of the cabin. Rico had held back, and now he followed in the sheriff's tracks, easily making the climb as well. Both vehicles nosed toward the cabin porch, where the skinny old man was pulling on a padded coat over his coveralls as he stepped out.

Evan stood behind his open door. "Lyle Bolton?"

The man stared hard. A woman wearing gray sweatpants and a bulky sweatshirt joined him, staying behind her husband's shoulder. These had to be the parents of Cindy Bolton. The daughter's description had been accurate as to her father's belligerence and mother's passivity.

"We've just got a couple questions," Evan said, moving forward as soon as he was certain the man wasn't armed. "I'd like to show you a picture. See if you know anything about this?"

Bolton held his stance at the top of the porch steps, leaving Evan the inferior position of standing below him. He pulled the photo from his pocket and handed it up.

Lyle barely gave it a glance. Nancy's eyes went wider for a moment before she adopted a puzzled expression and shook her head.

"Nope, never seen it," Lyle said, handing the photo back.

"You're absolutely certain about that? Take another look," Evan offered.

"Nope. Told you, I never seen that car."

To her right, Sam sensed Rico moving forward, positioning himself.

"Well, Mr. Bolton, that's a weird thing," Evan said, "because we've got the car in custody and we found your fingerprints in it. Can you explain that?"

Lyle practically flung his wife aside as he roared down the two steps toward the sheriff, arms flailing and spittle forming on his mouth. "You cops are all alike—trying to pin things on innocent citizens. I got my rights! You plant evidence and then come after me! Well, I ain't havin' it!"

Rico rushed into place, reaching for the handcuffs on his belt. With Bolton's right hand secured, he said, "Lyle Bolton, you're being detained for questioning in the matter of grand theft auto."

Evan stepped closer to the wriggling man. "Mr. Bolton, at this point we just need some answers about the car. You can make this easy by coming along to talk to us, or you can make it hard."

His eyes went to the porch, and Sam followed. Nancy Bolton was edging toward the screen door. Sam walked closer and signaled her to come forward, and Lyle seemed to notice her for the first time.

"You! I saw you casing my property the other day. It's a damn gov'ment conspiracy to spy on me, make up evidence, take away my rights!" He spun toward Evan again. "She's just another part of the whole frame-up!"

His feet skidded on the snowy ground as Evan and Rico took his arms and guided him toward Rico's cruiser.

"Nancy! Call Bennie and have him get holt of a lawyer. Let 'em know this is a civil rights issue. Damn cops are out to get me!"

The wife turned toward the door, but Sam was at her side now. "Later. He'll have plenty of time to get a lawyer."

While the men got their suspect situated in the cruiser, Sam turned to the woman. "I spoke to Cindy a few days ago."

Nancy's mouth went slack. "What? My daughter?"

"She asked me to drive by and see if things looked okay here. Are they? Okay, I mean?"

Nancy nodded. "Yeah, fine."

"You recognized that car in the photo, didn't you?" Sam kept her voice gentle, but the other woman closed up and shook her head again.

"Think about it. We need to know why your husband was in the car and how it got to where it was found. Just some simple answers. Please?"

But Nancy's eyes were on her husband as Rico backed the cruiser around and Lyle stared at his home pathetically from the side window.

"Sorry. Can't help you," Nancy said. She was shivering as she pulled the door open and went back inside.

Chapter 35

"Did you get anything from the wife?" Evan asked as they drove back to the station.

"Not a thing. She's lying about the car. That seemed evident the moment she saw the photo."

"I agree. She could be intimidated as hell by her husband. We see that a lot. Women more scared of him than of the law."

Sam leaned back in her seat. "I couldn't tell if it's that, or if she's in agreement with him about the whole 'government's out to get me' stuff. She did flinch when I mentioned her daughter's name."

Evan gave her a sideways look. "Do I know about *that*?"

"It was the connection that got me to drive up there a couple days ago. I told you about my bakery customer who knows the daughter who was raised in that cabin. She told me a little about the family, and I spoke to the daughter too. She's close to her mom but calls her dad a nutcase."

They were at a stop sign now, farther down the mountain. "And you didn't think to tell me all this?"

"I didn't know until an hour ago that Lyle Bolton's fingerprint was in Casey Hardwick's car *or* that Lyle had a record. Come on, Evan. None of us made that connection. It just hit me what a coincidence it is that a gingerbread house I made for Easter happened to look like the cabin where this couple lives."

Coincidence … Beau always said there were rarely coincidences in his work.

The book. It was telling them things, feeding them clues about the missing boys.

"… search warrant to see if we can find any evidence of the boys inside that cabin." Evan was going on, and Sam had the feeling she'd missed something. "Maybe you can get something out of the wife. Drop the daughter's name again and try to open a conversation?"

"Um, sure." Sam stared out the window as they passed through El Prado on their way into town. "Are you also bringing her in?"

"Sam, did you follow what all I just went through? I don't have a female deputy right now, and if we go back to that place with a warrant and the wife is there alone …"

"Right. Sure. Just give me a call when it's going to happen." In a day or two, most likely. Meanwhile, Evan could deal with Lisa Packard and try to come up with something to appease the families.

She retrieved her truck from the department lot and debated what to do next. It was getting late in the day—

okay, not really, but there was still plenty of slush on the streets and runoff that would freeze to treacherous levels soon after dark. She checked in by phone with Jen. All was well at Sweet's Sweets.

Sticking with the main streets where traffic had fairly well cleared the roadways, she headed north. Beau would have had his hands full, clearing the drive, tending the animals. Would she tell him the latest on the case? She wasn't sure. He missed his law enforcement days, and although he stuck by his assertion that he'd left the life behind, she often wondered. If presented with the chance to run for sheriff again, would he?

That train of thought was interrupted by her phone. She hit the hands-free button when she saw it was Kelly.

"Hey, what's up?"

"I'm a little freaked, Mom. There's something here I'd like you to see, if you have a chance on your way home."

"What is it?"

"You need to see it."

"Sure, I'll come." She'd already passed the turnoff to Kelly's place, but she found an easy enough spot to hook a U-turn and go back. "Be there in five minutes."

The Victorian looked like a picture postcard, with thick snow on the roof still, and icicles hanging from the eaves. The front porch had been shoveled, but Sam headed under the side portico and the back door.

Kelly met her, eyes a little wide, movements a bit jittery.

"Do I take off my coat, or not?"

"Sure. Sorry, hang it up. The kettle is hot if you'd like some tea."

"Maybe you'd better tell me about the thing that has you all spooked. Then we'll see about tea."

"Attic." Kelly led the way and unlocked the door. "I didn't want anyone coming along to mess this up." Eliza meowed as she trailed along.

"Where are Scott and Ana, anyway? The house seems quiet."

"They're doing some science experiment that involves snowflakes. I think they went out to the far back corner of the lot, but they could come home any time."

She opened the attic door and pointed to the trestle table. The leatherbound book lay open on top. Sam walked over to it and looked. The page on the righthand side showed a watercolor picture of a forest full of trees, laden with snow.

"It's kind of stark. I don't remember seeing it before."

"Because it wasn't there before," Kelly said, sounding a little shaky.

"Sweetie, we know the book changes all the time. We've found new pages bound into the thing at times. The cabin picture was one we'd never seen either."

"Mom, that's what I'm saying. Sorry I wasn't clear. This page is where the cabin picture was. Now it's a snowy scene. No cabin."

Sam started to riffle the pages. "Are you sure?"

"I am absolutely sure. When I opened the book, it fell to this page, just like it did before, to reveal the cabin to us." She took a deep breath. "I was startled, so I flipped through every single page. The cabin is gone."

Sam felt as if a cloud had just passed over. "It's telling us something."

Chapter 36

Sam reached for her phone in her pocket, but then hesitated. She should call Evan, but what was she going to tell him? A watercolor picture in a book wasn't going to get his attention. She set the phone down and rubbed her temple.

"Let's talk this through, see if we can figure out what it means. So, the book is telling us something. The picture of the cabin led me to ask questions about the cabin, and now we're learning that place might have been connected to the missing boys. You think the snowy forest is connected to them too?"

"Yes. I mean, *I* believe that. I'm not sure how to put it together, but if it turns out the cabin had something to do with them, does this new picture also have something to do with them? Their situation may have changed."

Sam drummed her fingers on the table top for a long moment. "I'm calling Evan."

The dispatcher told her he was in an interrogation with a man they'd brought in earlier. Standard policy was that interrogations were not to be interrupted.

"This may be related," Sam said. "Be sure you have him call me the minute he's done."

They heard sounds downstairs. "My family is back." Kelly closed the book and put it on the shelf.

Sam glanced out the attic window. Dusk was falling fast and the roads would only get worse. "I'm going to head home. I'll let you know what I hear from Evan."

She and Beau were finished with dinner and settling in front of the fireplace by the time the sheriff called.

"Sorry, Sam. Long day."

She'd been thinking about the new revelation all evening, and still didn't think it was a great idea to let Evan know her latest clue had come from a magical book. "What's the latest on getting a warrant for the cabin?"

"We got the paperwork in to the judge, but he'd left for the day. With Lyle in a holding cell for the night, I couldn't see a huge rush. I'll probably have it by morning."

"Yes, daylight would be good."

"We'll be looking for evidence that the boys are or ever were in the house, or any evidence that Lyle might have stashed the Mustang in his barn before he decided to take it to Questa."

"So, he admitted he took it there?"

"Not in so many words. He tries too hard to be cagey, but his attorney did come and advised him to tell us what he could about the car. The old guy basically just clammed up."

"Makes it seem like he has plenty to hide."

"I think so."

"I want to go along on the search," Sam said. "And we need to look in the forest around the house too."

"The forest ... okay. And I'd already planned to include you, for the reasons I told you earlier. You'll probably hear from me in the morning, maybe noon at the latest. Keep your fingers crossed."

It was going to be a sleepless night.

Chapter 37

Benjamin wasted two matches but finally got a handful of moss and pine needles to catch with the third. He had only one left. Carefully, he fed more pine needles to the flame, then the smallest of the few dry sticks he'd gathered. The largest branch that was halfway dry was only about the diameter of his wrist and he needed more, many more, if he had a prayer of keeping the fire going all night.

He looked toward the others. Casey had stopped shivering. That was a bad sign. Shivering was the body's way of generating heat, and when that stopped it could mean he was shutting down. Jacob had been asked to help look for dry wood, but for the past hour his fingers were so stiff he couldn't flex them. And now the tips were turning white. Also not a good sign.

"C'mon, you two. Get over here. It's a little warmer.

I'm going to look for more wood."

They had kept on the move most of the day, hopefully putting distance between themselves and the cabin. At one point around dawn, he questioned himself—had they crossed a highway during the worst of the blizzard? Had they missed their chance of locating an easy path to civilization? He had to put that thought aside.

He hadn't heard noises that would indicate Lyle was following them. But he figured the old man was a survivalist and would be crafty in the forest. He could probably sneak up on them and they'd never know it. But now he had to risk the light and the smell of a campfire. They would freeze to death otherwise.

Burrowing through the debris at the base of a large pine, where the snow was not nearly as deep, he came up with an entire fallen branch that wasn't in bad shape. He could break it into shorter lengths. He dragged it back to the sheltered spot where he'd left the others and felt his heart sink. Jacob looked up at him, apologetically.

"Sorry, man. I just tried to put on another stick. I don't know what happened."

The fire was out.

Benjamin fought back the urge to throttle him, to rant, to cry. He raised his eyes heavenward. *Please, oh, please … If we make it out of this alive, I swear I will never tell about that hidden room or the guns or the cash or anything about that place.*

He must have spoken the words out loud. Jacob and Casey were both nodding. "Me neither," they both said at once.

Benjamin closed his eyes for a second, reiterating the promise to whatever powers there were. Then he pulled out the matchbook with its one remaining little scrap of hope.

Chapter 38

The search warrant came through a little after nine in the morning. By the time Evan assembled a team and Sam joined them for the ride to the Bolton place, it was well after ten. Nancy Bolton met them at the front door, trying like crazy to present the same you-can't-touch-us attitude her husband exuded, but she wasn't Lyle. Sam was glad to see that.

Nancy scanned the warrant and stepped aside when Evan ordered her to. Two deputies headed toward the garage building, while the others spread out, starting with the bedrooms and bathrooms. Nancy started to trail along, jittery over the fact that so many people were invading her home. Evan gave Sam a nod, suggesting she take the woman to the kitchen. She noticed the place smelled like Lysol.

"Take fingerprints in each room," he instructed, ignoring the woman's protests. "The usual surfaces—light switches, doorknobs, faucet handles."

The department's forensic expert set to work on that, while the rest of the deputies poked through closets, dresser drawers, and medicine cabinets. Sam took Nancy by the arm and led her to the kitchen.

"How about a cup of tea?" she suggested. "Do you have a kettle?"

"Coffee's already made. Percolator."

Sam spotted it and turned on the burner beneath to rewarm it. Nancy brought two mugs out of a cupboard.

"How long will this take?" she asked, automatically reaching for the sugar bowl and going to the refrigerator for milk.

"I really don't know. I don't have a lot of experience with searches."

She remembered Beau talking about crime scenes that could take most of a day. But this wasn't necessarily a crime scene, she reminded herself, although she recalled the wording on the warrant allowed the men to look for signs of foul play. She really hoped it didn't come to that. She poured the brew into the two mugs and gestured toward the kitchen table, where they took seats.

The coffee was vile stuff that tasted as though it had been sitting for three days. After the first sip, Sam ignored her mug and reached into the inner pocket of her official jacket. Pulling out the photos of the three boys, she laid them on the table facing Nancy.

"Yesterday, the sheriff asked about a red car—their car," she began. "Take a look and tell me if you've seen any of these young men."

A glimmer of something crossed the woman's face, but she covered quickly by raising her mug and drinking. She closed her eyes and shook her head.

Sam left the photos in place. "Their families are *so* scared right now. Casey's mother is gravely ill." She ran a finger gently over Casey's face in the picture. "And Benjamin's mother has come to town."

She talked a bit about Lisa Packard, painting her as softer and more vulnerable than she'd actually come across.

"My family became involved because my daughter is a close friend of Casey's sister. She's the one who called us, nearly frantic."

Nancy sniffed, and Sam saw emotion that was barely contained beneath the surface.

"They're really worried that Casey won't get home to California in time to see his mother alive. So sad." Sam looked down at the pictures. "*So* sad."

When she looked up, a tear was rolling down Nancy's weathered face. The woman wiped it with the cuff of her sweater, just as the two deputies from the garage came into the house, stomping snow from their boots. Sam's moment to read Nancy was gone.

"Can you all at least wipe your feet outside?" she demanded. "I just mopped those floors."

Evan stepped out from a hallway and conferred quietly with the two, apparently learning they'd not found anything significant in the garage building.

Sam signaled him over. "Don't forget about the surrounding forest—what we talked about."

"Right." The sheriff turned to the other deputies. "Circle out from the house into the woods. You're looking for footprints. Maybe three sets. Or, if you don't spot those, look for one or two sets, any indication that these kids might have been carried away from this house."

The two men nodded and headed for the front door.

"And if there's any sign of digging, at all, you come and get me immediately."

Privately, Sam thought if there had been signs of footprints or digging it would have been completely covered with snow by now. She tried to remember the picture in the old book—did it show a disturbance on the ground? She wished she'd snapped a photo of it, but had been too distracted at the time.

A voice from another room called out to Evan and he left, clomping down some stairs somewhere, by the sound of it. Sam turned back to Nancy. The woman was staring at the photos of the missing men again, tense as a wire.

"Nancy?"

"No, I can't."

"Can't what? What do you know that you can't talk about?"

Nancy drained her mug, set it down, withdrew her hands to her lap. She hung her head.

"Nancy, something happened here, didn't it?" Sam kept her voice gentle. "I know you recognize these young men. Your husband said you'd never seen them, but that's not true, is it?"

"I- I can't."

"Nancy, you have to tell us. Please—the families are frantic. What's happened to the boys?"

"They were just so lost. I felt sorry for them. It seemed harmless to bring them in, give them some dinner …"

Sam felt an electric tingle go through her. Should she get Evan in here? Should she record what was about to be said? But she couldn't afford to spook this woman into silence; she kept quiet and let her talk.

"My husband took away all their things. I was to clean the house thoroughly. Unless I missed something, you won't find fingerprints. The basement wasn't the most comfortable room, but once they saw— I made them pancakes. The younger boy loved my pancakes."

What? Sam struggled to put it together, this disjointed narrative that seemed all out of whack. She wanted to take notes, but was afraid any movement would interrupt and Nancy would stop talking altogether. She concentrated on remembering enough key words and phrases to be able to relate this to Evan, hoping he would walk in quietly enough to be a party to the confession.

"… but the blizzard … and they were gone into the forest. Hoped they would just make it to town or a driver would pick them up." Nancy looked up at Sam. "No one picked them up, did they?"

Sam shook her head. "They're still missing." And the book had provided another valuable clue.

Lucidity returned. "I can't stand thinking of them, out there in the storm, lost in the woods. They left night before last. What can we do?"

Sam stood. "I'm going to bring the sheriff in. We need his help, and I need you to tell him everything, right from the beginning. But let's start with getting those young men to safety."

Chapter 39

Somehow, once the words search and rescue came up, everything became a flurry. Such missions were coordinated at the state level, through the state police, and that's who Evan called.

"We'll be assigned an incident commander, most likely from the state police office here in town. They'll call in the Taos SAR volunteers. It's an excellent group. And likely we'll draw on resources from other surrounding communities—Angel Fire and Red River, maybe." Evan related all this to Sam in a low voice, standing just outside the Bolton's kitchen doorway, keeping an eye on Nancy.

"I'm going to interview her here with a recorder, if she'll agree. If not, I'll transport her to the station."

"I'd suggest keeping her away from her husband. Under his influence, she's going to shut down."

"Agreed. I've already radioed the station and told them to hold Lyle in a cell. We're looking at a lot more serious charges if those boys didn't survive two nights out in the cold."

"What can I do to help?" Sam asked.

He shook his head. "Nothing, really. The SAR teams are highly organized. They don't want untrained helpers wandering around in the woods. The guys I sent out to scout around awhile ago … they've already reported finding no prints near the property. The wind that came through, along with the heavy snowfall, obliterated any trace."

"Is the search and rescue mission going to be completely futile, Evan?"

"No, no. Don't think that way. It quit snowing early enough in the day. If the kids are on the move, there'll be signs of them. I'd like to think they have some type of outdoor experience and would know how to leave signs, to do little things to help us spot them, but I don't hold a lot of hope for that. They're young. Too many kids these days spend their lives in front of screens and video games."

"I'll talk to Kelly, have her reach out to the sister again. Maybe she can tell us more about Casey and his friends."

"And Lisa Packard. See if you can catch her at the hotel or maybe the station, and see what she can tell you. Just be careful about how much you say about the rescue attempt. We can't promise anything, but it's okay to let her know we're moving ahead and getting right on this."

"Will do."

"I'll have Martinez give you a ride to town. I've requested a helicopter, and was assured they'd launch the one in Santa Fe. Should be here within the hour."

Sam walked back into the kitchen where Nancy Bolton

sat at the table, staring blankly at her mug of cold, nasty coffee. Tears were running unchecked down the woman's face.

"Nancy, thank you so much for telling us what's been going on. The sheriff is going to take your statement. Please tell him everything you can remember. Okay?"

Nancy nodded without making eye contact.

"You know, you could be credited with saving their lives," Sam said gently. "Thank you."

This was not the time to mention that both Boltons could also be blamed for the grave danger they'd put the young men in. Or worse, if the three were not found alive. At this moment, Sam had to hold out hope and they still needed Nancy's cooperation. She climbed into a cruiser and prayed as Deputy Martinez put the SUV in gear and drove the narrow road back toward the highway.

They arrived to find the Sheriff's Department building abuzz with the news. Reporters from the local newspaper and one radio station stood in the lobby, begging for a statement from the sheriff. The desk officer sent a questioning look toward Sam and the deputy. Martinez had been one who was tasked with searching the garage building at the Bolton place and knew nothing much beyond that. He nudged Sam forward. Oh boy. What to say?

She cleared her throat. "At this time there is little news, other than to say that Sheriff Evan Richards is in contact with state and county-wide search and rescue teams and a search has been initiated." Did that sound close enough to what Evan would say if he were here to do this?

"Where is the search focused?" Mike Garcia asked.

Martinez spoke up now. "Carson National Forest, in the Taos Ski Valley area. We can't be any more specific, sorry.

The roads are still not in great shape, and extra vehicles and civilians would only hamper the search efforts."

Hearing the commotion, two people walked out of the squad room. One was Lisa Packard. Sam edged away from the group and went to intercept her.

"What's going on?" Lisa demanded. "Are those reporters? Is there bad news?"

"Let's go to Evan's office and I can fill you in." Sam touched Lisa's elbow and ushered her back to the squad room.

Standing in Evan's office with the door closed she related that they had reason to believe the boys had been out in the elements for a couple of nights.

"Do any of them have any outdoors experience at all?" she asked.

"Benjamin was in scouts when he was younger—ten or twelve years old. They went on campouts, but I have no idea what they covered or how much he would remember now."

"And the others? Any idea?"

Lisa shook her head. "I'll call the other families and find out."

"Good idea." And a relief to hand off a task that would keep her busy for a few minutes.

Sam stepped back out into the squad room, leaving the office door standing open. Martinez had come back there and was talking to Rico at his desk.

"Mike from the *Taos News* said there will be more reporters here soon," Martinez was saying. "Scanners get the word out quick. What'll we do with them? You saw how crowded the lobby got with just a couple of them and their photographers."

Sam looked to Rico.

"Sheriff Beau sometimes set up a media center, somewhere off the premises, whenever there was a big case."

"Somewhere such as…?"

"Maybe a hotel suite or conference room. The Kachina Inn has some. I'll call over and see if there's a room available." Rico made the call and gave a thumbs up.

"Why don't we ask Mike to be the media coordinator," Sam suggested. "He'd be able to get the word out, tell new arrivals that's where they need to meet. Maybe the hotel could provide some coffee, whatever it takes to keep them out of your hair here and away from the actual search site."

"It's times like this I wish the department had a public relations coordinator," Rico said with a grin. "Sam, you want the job?"

"Oh, no, no. I'm fine with just being a baker."

Lisa Packard emerged from Evan's office, not looking hopeful. "Sorry. Both Casey's sister and Jacob's mom say the other two boys have no outdoor experience beyond watching girls on the beach. I'm afraid the southern California lifestyle doesn't teach any of us much about what to do in snowy conditions."

Sam tried to send her a comforting look. "We've got some of the best in the northern mountains on the job now. We're going to stay positive, okay?"

"Is it all right if I hang around here so I can get news as it comes in?"

Sam looked to Rico for an answer. He gave a tiny negative headshake.

"You'd be much more comfortable in your hotel," Sam said. "Really, the coffee here sucks and the lunches consist of vending machine snacks. While the deputies go out front to announce the plans for the reporters, you and I can sneak out the back way. It'll be better if they don't waylay you with a lot of questions."

She spotted Lisa's jacket laying on the back of a chair, and before anyone could argue with her suggestion, she'd plucked it up and handed it to the woman, taking her elbow and heading for the back door, which led to the employee parking area. From there, they'd skirt the outside of the outer wall and retrieve their own vehicles.

Once she'd seen Lisa safely into her rental Ford Explorer, Sam climbed into her truck. An idea had been nagging at her all morning, and it was time to take another look at that snowy painting in the book.

Chapter 40

Kelly had lunch on the table when Sam pulled in under the portico. "It's just soup and sandwiches, but I'll throw together another one if you haven't eaten yet," she said when Sam walked into the kitchen.

The scent of buttery bread with grilled cheese made her mouth water. "I can't really remember the last time I ate, so yes. Yes, please."

Scott had nearly finished his sandwich, and Ana left hers sitting on the plate as she rushed over to grip Sam around the legs. "We're studying bugs!" she announced.

"Spiders and other arachnids," Scott clarified. "Based on the little guys we caught building webs across Mommy's washing machine."

"That is *not* a reflection on how seldom I do laundry," Kelly insisted, flipping Sam's sandwich to brown the other side. "Those pesky critters can make a sizeable web overnight."

"Back to your lunch, kiddo," Scott said, tapping the table beside Ana's soup bowl. "We have to finish our research and learn exactly what type of spider we have. And then we need to carefully carry him outside so he can start a new web in the bushes or somewhere more appropriate than our laundry room."

"Yes, thank you." Kelly cut the hot sandwich in half and ladled soup into a bowl.

She and Sam settled at the table. Ana announced she was already full, so Scott cleared their places and told Ana they could go. They left through the butler's pantry and took the back stairs to the second floor.

"There was something on the radio this morning about a search and rescue mission to find the missing boys," Kelly said, testing her soup and deciding to microwave it a few seconds.

"Yeah, it's getting underway now. In fact, the helicopter ought to be here from Santa Fe already. We learned that the three had been in that same cabin I drove by the other day. It gives me the shivers to know I was that close. If I'd just seen one of their faces at the window or something."

"I think you mentioned a search warrant for the house?"

"The husband is in custody and the wife was there. I started talking to her and bits of the story came out. Evan is still getting her statement. I gather they were holding the boys in the basement and they escaped."

"So, see? You wouldn't have seen them looking out a window, even if they'd realized you were there."

"And I'm not exactly clear on when they escaped the

cabin and started out into the woods, but it sounds like it was the night of the blizzard."

"Remember the day I felt really strange? Maybe I was getting some kind of vibe from them, like they were planning the escape, or maybe they were already out in the wild by then."

"It's been eating at me. I really should have pulled on up to that cabin and confronted the old man. His stare was almost ferocious, well, challenging. I turned around and left, and that might have been the move that sealed the fate of those kids." She'd set down her spoon and was nibbling at a tiny piece of the bread crust.

"Mom, you can't blame yourself for *anything*. It's just been a weird set of circumstances."

"I want to take another look at the book. If it hasn't vanished, I need to know more details from the snowy forest scene you found in there."

"Absolutely. Do you think the picture changes as new events happen?" Kelly paused with her sandwich triangle midway to her mouth. "What am I saying—of course it does. We already know it changed from showing us the cabin to revealing the forest."

They finished their lunches in a couple more bites and hurried up to the third floor. Once Kelly closed the door behind them, with the cat close on her heels, she pulled the leatherbound book from the shelf. Eliza jumped to the window seat.

Sam held her breath, hoping like crazy that the snowy forest picture hadn't vanished entirely.

It hadn't. Kelly turned a couple of the old, parchment-like pages and there it was.

"I didn't pay enough attention to the details last time,"

Sam admitted. "Let's get more light on this."

Kelly carried the book to the bay window and they edged the cat aside so they could both sit.

"There's a clue—footprints," Sam pointed out.

"Three sets. I wish I'd noticed them the last time."

Sam ran a finger over the footprints as they led deeper into the forest. Suddenly, she stopped. "Would you say that's a campfire? That little blob of orangey-red."

"Could be. Yes, I'd say definitely."

The scene appeared to dim. Sam looked outside to see if a cloud had covered the sun, but light and shadows outdoors were unchanged. She looked at Kelly, whose eyes were wide.

"You're not wrong. The picture is getting darker and the fire is getting brighter, as if it's nightfall. Holy cow!"

"Is it showing what happened last night, do you think? Or is this the prediction for tonight?"

Kelly rubbed at her forearms. "This is giving me goosebumps."

Abruptly, the tiny orange fire went out.

"Oh no." Sam grabbed the book and held it closer to the light. There was no sign of the little bright spot, and the forest continued to dim until it appeared as a gray-on-gray representation of a night scene.

"Without their campfire, they'll freeze," Kelly whispered.

Sam raised her gaze to the high beamed ceiling. "I really wish the picture was a map, showing us exactly where this scene really is."

Kelly seized upon the idea. "Let's look."

She carefully turned every page to the end of the book, then started again at the beginning and went through each one. No other drawings appeared, only the strange rune-like writing that always filled the book. They spent the next two hours taking turns handling the carved box, then reading the revealed text. But there was nothing in the book about the missing young men.

The picture remained dark.

Chapter 41

S am felt at loose ends. Go home, stay at Kelly's, go back to the station, go bake some brownies? Baking always provided an excellent distraction, so the brownie idea began to feel better and better. She drove to Sweet's Sweets and filled their largest pan with batter.

Ninety minutes later she realized the bakery couldn't possibly sell all this, and she didn't dare leave herself alone with the gooey treats, so she filled two boxes and took them to the sheriff's department. Her timing was excellent. All the deputies from this morning's search had just come in, and the squad room had turned into a noisy crowded roomful of volunteers as it became the incident command center for the SAR operation. The brownies began to disappear with record speed.

No news from the SAR field teams, according to Rico.

The ground teams had not come across any trace of the guys, but between the Wheeler Peak Wilderness and Taos Ski Valley itself, there were nearly 20,000 acres where they could have ended up. The helicopter had flown to the airport to refuel and would keep flying a grid pattern until it became too dark out to see anything.

Sam thought of the picture in the book, dimming into a night scene, and her own tension level revved back up again. She had a bad feeling that a third night out on the mountain would not end well for the three young men.

She found a quiet corner in the ladies restroom and phoned Kelly.

"Hi, Mom. Yeah, I've been back through the book and nothing has changed. The picture shows night coming on, but nothing gives a clue about those guys' whereabouts."

Sam could hear Ana in the background and "peanut butter" repeated in that repetitive way little kids have of nagging their parents.

"I'd better get some dinner started or this girl's going to make her own sandwich. I'll check the book again later this evening."

When the call ended she dialed Beau.

"Hey, hon, what's up?" He sounded a little breathless and explained he'd just stepped inside after shoveling the large back deck.

She recapped the day so far. "We don't know anything and it seems like the search isn't netting much information."

"They often go that way. I've been involved in searches that took days."

"That isn't exactly reassuring. The kids have been out in the elements for two nights already. I'm worried about that."

"I know, Sam. Listen, the dogs and I are fine here at home. Just hang out at the station if you want to. Lend a hand if that makes you feel better. I'm sure Evan and the SAR commander can use extra people for all types of duties."

"He does seem to be running sort of ragged," she said, remembering the sheriff behind his glassed-in office. There had been a steady parade of people in and out since he'd returned.

She thanked Beau for his understanding and ended the call. Outside the little bathroom sanctuary, the noise level had picked up and she went to see what was happening. Nothing new, it seemed. Frustration hung over everyone.

Another fifteen minutes went by before Evan stood and stretched, looking like someone who would kill for a bathroom break. But at the moment, the wife of the radio station's manager showed up with a huge pan full of tamales. "Don't get mad, Sheriff. Ronnie told me about the search, and I know people get hungry. Take these, for anyone who wants something to eat."

He smiled and thanked her, signaling for Sam to carry the food to the crowded squad room. Sam waylaid the food donor and thanked her profusely, inviting her to bring her homemade tamales into the busy room, making chit-chat long enough to allow Evan to escape down the hall.

Once the woman left, Sam wandered down to the interrogation section, but the two rooms and the monitoring center between them were dark and quiet. Evan stepped out of the men's room just then, his shoulder radio crackling with a staticky voice. He turned toward the end of the hall and responded. A minute later he walked back toward Sam.

"No news from the ground coordinator," he said with a shake of his head.

"That's not good." Sam glanced toward the clock at the end of the hall. "It'll be too dark to fly pretty soon."

His mouth quirked in a grimace as if to say, thanks for stating the obvious.

"Evan, would it do any good to talk to Lyle Bolton again? See if he'd cooperate and reveal anything about the direction the boys might have gone?"

"I doubt it. First off, the guy has lawyered up and I'm sure has been advised not to say anything at all. Not that he was talking to us anyway."

"If he knew Nancy had already talked with us? Maybe that would break down his defensive attitude and he might come up with ..." She had no idea what she hoped for.

Evan shook his head slowly. "I wouldn't. We don't know enough about this Bolton guy yet, other than he holds a lot of anger. If he thought his wife betrayed him ... no, that wouldn't be good. It's going to come out soon enough anyway, but I can't put her in jeopardy if his lawyer actually convinces the judge to grant bail in the morning."

Everything he said made sense, but it left Sam wandering and watching the clock. It only took a few minutes of that to convince her to volunteer to help Rico in any way she could.

"Sam," he said, "it's frustrating, I know. Not being in the middle of the action, feeling like we're doing nothing, waiting for news. It makes me want to ... pace the floor."

"I was going to say, it makes me want to scream," she said with a smile. "But I suppose that wouldn't be a good idea, not in here."

"Right."

So, she went back to watching the clock. For once she was glad for the early start of Daylight Savings Time. They would have one more hour of light, but not much beyond that, especially for flight operations over the forest. Sam clenched her fists so tightly she felt the nails dig into her palms. She *hated* feeling so helpless.

Rather than taking a share of the food provided for the volunteers, Sam decided to take a quick walk down to the Sidewalk Café and get something for herself. Part of her weariness was from the lack of solid protein and the steady input of caffeine and sugar ever since she'd made the brownies. Plus, the fresh air would surely perk up her spirits.

The little mom-and-pop place was only a block from the station. She and Beau had eaten there many times when he found short breaks from his sheriff duties. The girl behind the counter was a daughter of the owners and she recognized Sam right away.

"Let me guess—a turkey and Swiss on whole wheat?"

Sam chuckled. "You know me too well. Plus, chips and an extra wedge of dill pickle."

"You got it." She walked around to the work table, slipped on plastic gloves and began making the sandwich. "I heard about the search for those college kids. Are you helping with that?"

"I wish. I've been sitting on the sidelines and feeling useless."

"Trekking through the woods in snow up to your hips isn't for anyone but the real athletes. Not that I'm saying you couldn't handle it …"

"No, you're right. It's a tough assignment." Sam reached

for the bag with her dinner. "Say some prayers."

"We all are."

Sam took a deep breath of the late afternoon air, watching for potentially icy patches on the sidewalk, walking back to the chaotic station at a leisurely stroll. She really should have made the rounds of the deputies and asked if anyone else wanted food, but it seemed the donated tamales had filled most of the need.

When she walked back into the squad room, it was immediately apparent something had changed. People were all facing the incident commander who had a phone to his ear, and a feeling pervaded, of two dozen breaths being held.

"What's their condition?" A long pause. "Keep me posted."

He stood and held up his hands to quiet the murmur that ran through the room.

"The helicopter spotted them. They were able to land in a clearing fairly close by and EMTs hiked to the subjects. They're not in good shape, but they are now aboard the aircraft and being transported to the hospital."

Chapter 42

Sam?" Evan Richards was standing at her shoulder. "Lisa Packard needs to get this news personally, so I'm heading over to her hotel. I'd appreciate your riding along, if you don't mind. You seemed to have a better rapport with her than some of the others. The situation may be helped by a woman's touch."

"Sure. Happy to." She was still holding the bag with her supper.

"Bring it along. I have no rules against eating in my cruiser."

"Maybe it would be better if I offered it to Lisa," Sam said as they walked out the back door.

"We'll see how the evening unfolds." He unlocked the vehicle and they climbed in, taking advantage of his flashing lights to move quickly through the traffic near the plaza. At the turn-in to the hotel, he killed the lights. Pulling up in front of Lisa's room was going to be traumatic enough without the extra hoopla.

"Sheriff." The woman was as tightly wound as a brand new watch when she saw who was at the door.

"It's good news," he said, and Sam watched her posture droop with relief. Evan held up a hand. "I don't know *how* good. Search and rescue reports that they found all three boys and they are being airlifted to the hospital. They've probably arrived by now. We should go. Depending on their condition, doctors might make the choice to take them on to the regional trauma center in Albuquerque."

Lisa turned to grab her jacket and purse.

"You can ride with us or follow in your own car," he offered.

"I'd better ride with you. My whole body is trembling right now."

Sam gave her an encouraging smile. "You're holding together remarkably well."

The ten-minute ride took three, with Evan's lights and siren blaring. They drove directly to the emergency entrance where the helicopter sat forty feet away on the pad. Two EMTs were wheeling a gurney into the building.

Evan left the cruiser at the curb and the three of them rushed toward the gurney. The patient was covered in blankets, with only the center of his face showing. An IV line ran under the covers. Lisa studied the little bit she could see and shook her head. Not Benjamin.

"My son is here," Lisa cried out to the first person they encountered inside the bustling ER. "Benjamin Packard is one of the three just brought in."

"Yes, ma'am. Doctors are working on all the young

men. You won't be able to see him just yet." The nurse gently took Lisa's arm and led her down a corridor, saying something about forms to fill out.

Sam and Evan exchanged a look. They could probably learn more by acting like mice in the corner.

A lot of medical jargon was being tossed around as teams of two and three surrounded each of the three beds. Small peeks showed that the boys' clothing had been cut off, layers of blankets covered them, and IV lines and monitors were being attached. From what Sam could tell, the gurney they had followed, the last of the three, held the most serious case. A doctor emerged from that curtained cubicle and stopped short at the sight of the sheriff.

"These are the three missing kids, aren't they? Can you identify them for us? Wherever they've been, they left without wallets, phones, or any of the normal stuff."

"We can answer some of it. Sam? You know the faces well."

She remembered the photos she had shown to Nancy Bolton, in what seemed like another era. She pulled them out now and handed them to the doctor, one by one, giving the names.

"Will they make it, doctor?" Evan asked. "One of the mothers is here. We need to be prepared for her reaction."

The doctor nodded solemnly. "For what they've been through, according to the news, I'd say they're doing remarkably well. They've all got some degree of hypothermia. This kid," pointing to Casey's photo, "is in the worst shape. He's pretty cold. But we've got all the emergency treatments in place and we should see them all warming up within the next few hours."

"Hours?" Evan asked.

"We have to warm them very slowly or it can trigger other conditions, including heart attack." He saw alarm on their faces. "But they've got youth on their side. I'd say they'll end up being fine."

"I'm going to get the word out to the SAR teams and my department. I'd rather have the facts than a lot of speculation going around." Evan stepped over to a quiet corner and pulled out his phone.

Sam saw Lisa coming toward them and flashed her a smile before pointing her out to the doctor, to let him officially deliver the good news. She walked away from the bustling area and phoned Kelly.

Chapter 43

Two days later, Benjamin Packard was being touted as the hero of the day for his outdoor skills and doing his best to keep the others protected from the elements. Sam lingered over coffee with Beau in their living room, the two dogs curled at their feet, the TV turned on. Practically the moment the sheriff's department had released the announcement that the three young men had been rescued, the story took on epic proportions, with TV news crews from Albuquerque, Denver, and Phoenix converging on the hospital in Taos. The story spread to the national networks and it led the feel-good section of every newscast, once the more grisly news got exhausted.

"It's amazing to think that I never actually met the guys," Sam said.

"You were smart to stay away from the hospital. All

that hubbub."

"I know. The doctors wanted the boys to have complete rest while they observed them. I didn't need to be there to disrupt that."

"Evan's done a good job with the PR aspect of it," Beau commented. "I always hated that part, talking to the media about a big case, deciding how much or little to reveal."

Sam nodded. She'd spoken to Evan the morning after the dramatic rescue. Once they knew the boys were safe and would survive, it was now a question of how far to press charges against the Boltons. Nancy still swore they were only trying to help the kids who'd gotten lost. Lyle still said nothing. And the boys were curiously silent on the experience, other than to express how happy they were to be warm again.

The world might never know what they'd endured during the days in the Bolton cabin, although the doctors assured the sheriff that a complete physical exam revealed no injuries or signs of abuse. If there was no evidence of abuse and if the families didn't want to press charges, most likely there would be no legal case. The prosecutor surely wouldn't want to drag Nancy Bolton into court, the woman who tended to reminisce about making pancakes for three lost kids.

Sam's phone rang, and she set her coffee cup on the end table to answer. The name on the readout showed Lisa Packard.

"Lisa! How is everything going?"

"I just wanted to call and thank you. Please pass that along to Sheriff Richards and the search and rescue teams as well. I guess the department is jammed with calls. I haven't been able to get through. I'll be sending a written thanks once we're settled in at home again."

"I'm sure the scene at the hospital night before last was enough to let Evan know how grateful everyone is," Sam told her, recalling the tears and hugs, the obvious rush of joy everyone felt. "I hear the boys are being released today."

"Yes, we're checking out now. I'm trying to keep it low key, but there are still lots of news people hanging around outside. We'll drive to Albuquerque, and Southwest Airlines has comp'd us four tickets back to L.A."

"I guess Casey's car is still being held by the county. Would you like for me to check on that, figure out how to get it back to him?"

"That would be great. I hadn't actually thought of it."

"You've had a lot to deal with. How are the other families handling everything?"

"Jacob's parents are beside themselves, of course. They'll meet us at the airport when we arrive in L.A. Casey's mother is still not doing well, but it seems the news that he'll be home soon has given her a little boost. They expect there will be some time together for them."

Sam felt her eyes prickle. It was so good to hear that news.

"I had a surprise from the sheriff yesterday afternoon. He called to ask if the woman at the cabin where the boys stayed could come to the hospital for a short visit. He said he would escort her."

"Really?" Sam pictured Nancy Bolton as she'd broken down during their last chat. "What did you say?"

"I asked Benjamin and the other guys if that would be okay, and they all agreed, so I told the sheriff to bring her in. Of course, by the time they actually arrived all three boys were asleep. She insisted that I not wake them. She only wanted to look in and feel assured they were all right."

"That was nice. I spoke with her when they were searching her home. She seemed genuinely to care about the kids' welfare."

"Yes, I thought so too. But there was an even bigger surprise. While we were alone in Benjamin's room, Mrs. Bolton pulled a paper lunch sack out of her purse and handed it to me. 'To help out, for all the trouble we caused,' is what she said. When I opened the bag, I saw it was stuffed with cash."

"Wow. Wonder where she came up with that?"

"I have no idea, and I didn't get the chance to ask her. When I looked up again, she'd gone. I was simply too stunned to chase after her. Sam, it's plenty to cover the hospital expenses and to have Casey's car shipped home, and maybe other things."

"That's good. I got the definite feeling Nancy regretted how things turned out, that she never intended the boys any harm or to scare them." She didn't mention her doubts about the husband. Had Lyle threatened the boys in some way? Would they ever talk about it?

"Well, I need to get organized. I've got my own things from the hotel, and now I need to get the boys' stuff ready. I'm hoping to get out of here and on the road quietly but who knows how that will go."

"Good luck with it, and wish the guys well from all of us, okay?"

They'd barely said goodbye when Sam's phone rang again. Kelly wanted to check on the status of the young men. She'd already spoken with her friend Summer so she knew most of what Lisa Packard had just told Sam. Through Evan, she knew that Lyle Bolton would be facing charges for stealing the Mustang—a third- or fourth-degree felony in the state. Considering that the car was recovered undamaged, the punishment would probably amount to a fairly short jail sentence, if anything.

"One surprising thing," Kelly said. "Evan told me the Boltons' daughter came up here to talk to him. She was asking for leniency for her dad."

"My impression was they had nothing to do with each other."

"I know, right? She told Evan that Lyle has some big paranoia issues but he's basically not an evil person. She doubts the guys were ever seriously in danger in that house."

"Sounds like a daughter who had battles with a parent, but she's looking at it in a more mature way now."

Kelly chuckled a little. "I think we all know someone who could fit that description."

When the phone rang for a third time, Beau stood up and gathered their coffee mugs, heading for the kitchen. He had postponed his ranch chores long enough. This time, when Sam looked at the phone screen, she saw it was Rupert.

"Great news, girl," he said. "I've got my story rolling. My writer's block is gone!"

"I'm *so* happy to hear that." Actually, she was more relieved at the light tone of his voice. "Is it following the lines of what we talked about—the missing kids?"

"No, couldn't do that. Now that it's been all over the news, everyone will just think I borrowed a tired plotline. It's something else, and it'll thrill my historical romance fans. And that's all I can say for now."

"Good for you. I'll be eager to read it when it comes out."

"You know you don't have to. Romance isn't your thing. I just appreciate your being there for me when things were rough."

"Don't mention it. Anything for my buddy."

They ended the call. Sam glanced at the TV, where live coverage showed the exterior of the hospital in Taos, a crowd with cameras and microphones waiting for the doors to open. Oh boy. Then she spotted Evan's cruiser, pulling slowly away from the emergency entrance, no lights or fanfare, just a law enforcement vehicle driving along. And behind it, a white SUV. She couldn't tell if there were four people in it, but she liked to imagine there were.

Thank you for taking the time to read *Tricky Sweet*. If you enjoyed it, please consider telling your friends or posting a short review. Word of mouth is an author's best friend and is much appreciated.

Thank you,

Connie Shelton

Author's Note

A huge thanks to my editor, Stephanie Dewey, and to my beta readers who catch the many little things that my eyes miss: Marcia, Sandra, Susan, Isobel, Paula, and Judi—you are the best!

Sign up for Connie Shelton's free mystery newsletter at connieshelton.com
and receive advance information about new books, along with a chance at prizes, discounts and other mystery news!

Contact by email: connie@connieshelton.com
Follow Connie Shelton on Twitter, Pinterest and Facebook

* * *

Books by Connie Shelton

The Charlie Parker Series
Deadly Gamble
Vacations Can Be Murder
Partnerships Can Be Murder
Small Towns Can Be Murder
Memories Can Be Murder
Honeymoons Can Be Murder
Reunions Can Be Murder
Competition Can Be Murder
Balloons Can Be Murder
Obsessions Can Be Murder
Gossip Can Be Murder
Stardom Can Be Murder
Phantoms Can Be Murder
Buried Secrets Can Be Murder
Legends Can Be Murder
Weddings Can Be Murder
Alibis Can Be Murder
Escapes Can Be Murder
Old Bones Can Be Murder
Sweethearts Can Be Murder
Money Can Be Murder
Holidays Can Be Murder - a Christmas novella

The Samantha Sweet Series

Sweet Masterpiece
Sweet's Sweets
Sweet Holidays
Sweet Hearts
Bitter Sweet
Sweets Galore
Sweets Begorra
Sweet Payback
Sweet Somethings
Sweets Forgotten
Spooky Sweet
Sticky Sweet
Sweet Magic
Deadly Sweet Dreams
The Ghost of Christmas Sweet
Tricky Sweet
Spellbound Sweets – a Halloween novella
The Woodcarver's Secret

The Heist Ladies Series

Diamonds Aren't Forever
The Trophy Wife Exchange
Movie Mogul Mama
Homeless in Heaven
Show Me the Money

Children's Books

Daisy and Maisie and the Great Lizard Hunt
Daisy and Maisie and the Lost Kitten